Whose?

Other publications by Michael Glover

Poetry:
Measured Lives (1994)
Impossible Horizons (1995)
A Small Modicum of Folly (1997)
The Bead-Eyed Man (1999)
Amidst All This Debris (2001)
For the Sheer Hell of Living (2008)
Only So Much (2011)
Hypothetical May Morning (2018)
Messages to Federico (2018)
What You Do With Days (2019)

Others:
The Trapper (2008)
Headlong into Pennilessness (2011)
Great Works: Encounters with Art (2016)
Playing Out in the Wireless Days (2017)
111 Places in Sheffield You Should Not Miss (2017)
Late Days (2018)
Neo Rauch (2019)
The Book of Extremities (2019)
Thrust (2019)
John Ruskin: an idiosyncratic dictionary (2019)
Rose Wylie (2020)

As editor or contributor:

Memories of Duveen Brothers (1976)
Goin' down, down, down: Matthew Ronay (2006)
Between Eagles and Pioneers: Georg Baselitz (2011)
Robert Therrien (2016)
Monique Frydman (2017)

Whose?

A monologue
of posthumous days

Michael Glover

Whose? is being adapted for the stage by
Haste Theatre

www.1889books.co.uk

ISBN: 978-1-9996440-9-3

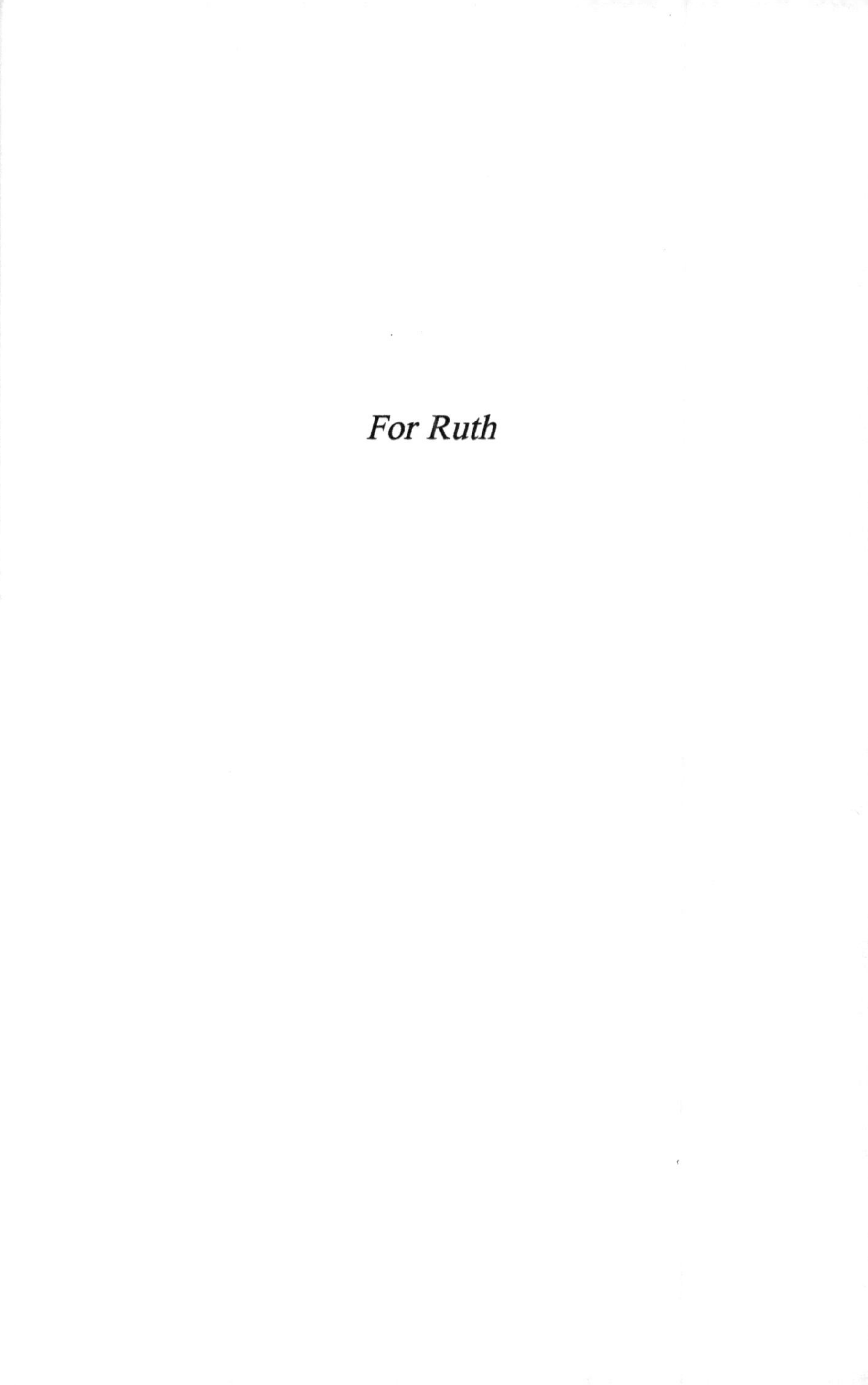

For Ruth

You idiot! You bone-head! But that's how it was. What else do you expect me to say? You contracted me for such and such a rate of pay, and now I am here, as you asked me to be, on a Thursday evening, fully prepared, wits about me. The props were all your business. You could say that *I* am the props – or, at the very least, quite as many of them as are needed. I have not asked for more. We never discussed it. We signed it, the two us, rather hurriedly because you – we both – needed to get on, and that was that. I barely skim these things these days because one is so much like another, all blah blah blah. Comic in its own way. Were it not sad, which it is. Paper – flittery, air-borne paper – seldom summarises anything adequately. It's the voicing, the voicing – the aaaahs, the ooooohs – I specialise in, the bringing it over, in a mad, bad, sad, oh so sad, world of total incomprehension and befuddlement, although I always hesitate to say that to you because you are always so serious, and you do seem to *believe* in it, regrettably.

Yes, I do agree – how could I not? – that at the entrance I stopped, as if frozen in mid-step. I looked about. There was bewilderment in my face. I do grant you that. It is called a pause, and even an *over-long pause*. You are about to begin, and then you pause, and you express regret, of sorts, perhaps for this life that you have lived, its untidiness, its mess, its lack of satisfactory completion, its multiplicity of loose ends. That is what it is. Full stop. It is what you would expect of a man such as myself. And, more to the point, it is all in the script. It is all in *this script*. The whole thing is scripted, from beginning to end. There is no foolishness of any kind. It is not even *off the wall* – whatever that might mean. It is entirely on the wall, pinned to it, all the words you are hearing me say now, it is all an integral part of it. Which is not to say that you will not take exception to some of it, find it rather, say, rebarbative. My life, my entire lived experience, has been rebarbative. Have you not noticed that? In fact, were you not the first – or one of them at the very least – to point it out? Was I not *rebarbative* when I first strutted into your office, hackles already rising, too cocksure for words? I was. I was. I was intolerable. And I have not changed much in the intervening years. And so I stand here for a while – this is how it goes, how it comes and goes, always – on this spot where I am standing now, and you contemplate my presence, alone of course, as we are all quite alone by now, by the stage in life that I have reached, quite far, you must understand. That is the whole point of it, to get to grips with this particular moment, to empty it all out, as one might empty out rats from a sack, all the ongoing unpleasantness of it all, the fudge, the fuss, the impotent fury, punctuated, of course, by these sweet, brief interludes of meditative calm, little tra la las, small, soothing hums and haahs...

The point is that I do not lack for energy, not yet. I am blowing off steam from all orifices! And that, if you like, can be part of the comedy of it all – if you like. I do still need your help from time to time. I am not entirely self-nurtured, self-propelled. You could even say that I need your encouragement, your guidance. You have always done that. You have always been part of the set, have you not? Should it be here or here or here? The whole thing is minimal, of course. Who wants to transport cumbersome sets around the country? That, however, does not detract from the problem of what exactly should be done with this box, the one in which I am scripted to stand here from time to time, as if frozen in time – as you once were – when I am not in fact standing in it. Because it is entirely illusory, of course. Should I kick it aside in fury or impatience? Or will someone run in from the wings – like a ball boy at Wimbledon – to snatch it up, make it vanish, make its symbolic significance entirely forgettable? There is a difference. A single glance makes such a difference. It changes me, on an instant, into someone else. The question, I suppose, is this: how many does any one of us need to be? How many have there been in our lives? Should we try to count? We know all about the tinker and the tailor and the beggarman and the thief, but how many more are waiting there in the shadows to hustle the latest one aside? So much is ever-renewing. You might also say, on a more sombre note, that there are far too many corpses strewn around. And what sort of an impact might all this have on our general sanity, do you think? I jest of course. It's all so much child's play in the end, so much juggling with hoops and balls, yellow hoops, red balls, on the sand before the ice cream van arrives with its jangly tune. The joyous white smear of the clown's mouth! The fact is that we hold it all in. We are English after all, one and all. We are drowned pearls of the sea, maestro, are we not? Let me walk off then for a moment, quite briskly, with a cheery wave of the swervy wrist. That should sort it all out. Until next time. If there is to be a next time.

I am not prepared to be coerced. There has been

no adequate preparation. I have not met you before. This space is new to me. I cannot judge the distance between this point where I am standing and the edge of the room, over there, beside the door by which I entered just now for the very first time in my life. Surely you must understand all that. After all, you are part of it in so far as you are here at all. And I do see you! It is as if I am a new-born today with all the marvellousness and all the terror of the completely unknown, the unfathomable. The trouble is that, like any new born, I am also entirely helpless, and perhaps even under-developed – at the very moment when you seem to be expecting so much of me. You have pushed me out here, and you have said to me: get on with it. You agreed. This is the time when it happens, you cannot renege on a contract. Contracts are firm. Contracts are binding. We have your signature on this piece of paper. But paper resembles a butterfly, does it not? You fold it up, you shape it in a certain way, and then you fling it away, and it flies through the air, away from you. And, in time, you lose sight of it altogether.

When you thin down like that, to a droplet, to a sort of shimmery translucency, it all goes so strange on me, the orchestra too, through which I walk, to magnificent applause of course, from all sides, holding up the wings of my coat, like so... It was as if I had never had it before. I was as if made anew by it, almost inventing myself again. You see, I *was* the choreographer, a choreographer without credits needless to say, but the choreographer all the same. Had you thought otherwise? Was it all your doing, in your opinion? Am I nothing then but a man of your making? Did you go that far? Is that what you told all your friends, here today, gone tomorrow, always hurrying out of the door, never quite entering? I wouldn't be surprised. Nothing surprises me now that the sea wall has collapsed and left the trains stranded. We both embraced Devon, for decades. The soil down a country lane, almost ravine-like! – with all that dull red blood running. You merely stood by, in the wings, and egged me on from time to time – when, that is – correction please! – you did not turn aside, as you so often did, because my silly antics bored you, as you always said. And you meant it. You should have seen the look on your face. I peeled it away just then as one tears away the cardboard wrapping around a book these days. It is the whole of excitement, to rend a small box, to take it out on something quite as harmless and useless as a box. And it is entirely repeatable, day after day, if there is cash in the bank. Be so lucky, my friend! Go for it, as my daughter might say. She was so small and so angry when they held her up that first time. Did I weep? Did you? There was mist, certainly, sea fog in the Channel, with the boats plying back and forth, and we were looking, and pointing, weren't we? And we were, just then, entirely happy.

Would you have begun in this way? Tell me. I need a little help, an arm perhaps to steady me. Or if not now, when? To career down the slope that afternoon, arms spread so wide, and even singing – or perhaps howling. *You choose,* my friend, my dear, old, some-time friend on the second row, you choose one of the many opportunities. There is a little tray here, bursting with goodies, heaped high with them. Sweeties for the sucking... The pier is just over there, and I am standing here as usual, waiting once again for you to finish whatever it is that you are doing – well, I ask you, why change things now? It has always been like this – being blown about as usual, hither and thither like a screwed up paper bag. The truth is that I am sick unto death of them all on this grey November Thursday when she has just walked by in that time-honoured fashion of hers, foot-slogging, with so little apparent concern, and that nose of hers at such a supercilious angle. The mere force of habit keeps us going. Don't look at me like that for god's sake! Show a little respect for a change. I may be older than your father. I challenge you to count the years. However many hands you choose to use. Don't be so coarse. Don't be so brazen.

There is always a moment – it comes to all of us, irrespective of race, class, religion and all the other what-nots – when you take someone aside and point out everything – everything that has gone wrong. And there is always so much of it, and it takes hours, days, of patient recitation, probably from a book, because it is far too long and involved – like a twisty rope, left out too long in the rain, behind the house, you know it, you have seen it with your own eyes – to commit to memory, even for an old hand such as myself. You completely and utterly exhaust yourself in the doing, you end up speechless, breathless, spent. I do anyway. One cannot walk away from one's nature. One is always there at the end of the day, waiting, tittering more like, thumbing a nose. That's how it is. And there is no other way. There is no other way back to the beginning. It is a very long climb, boots, crampons, the lot. And that is what I did to you, and you did not thank me for it, and so I left, almost immediately, without a coat, and it was chilly in the extreme. I almost caught my death. I lay full length on the pavement outside the butcher's shop, and beat down with my fists and just, well, wept. Those who saw it and called me mad failed to take into account the simple fact that I was being perfectly reasonable. Those who carried me away, rather brusquely – I was so much dead weight in my fury – were not even listening. I do not count them amongst my friends, of whom there are fewer and fewer these days. Only the men of faith remain, with whom I have a compact. Solemn. Solid. Let's not go into that.

An element of doubt enters in. It is always the spoiler. What next then? You remember, clearly. You can no longer rid yourself of that memory. It is too high to leap. Your arm was held at a certain height above your head, and you were about to speak the words in a certain order. And then the sea water washed in and lifted the scrabble board beyond your reach, and everything went away, the short words, the medium, the long. They passed beyond your reach, and your mouth was struck dumb, in the market place, where you had looked up once, and met the eye which transfixed you. Whose? Had you hurried away just then, had the

timing been right – and it is all down to timing –
you would never have suffered such consequences.
There is no one else to blame. To walk away now
would be utterly, utterly futile. It would be you
and you alone.

I understand what you are saying. It is what you
are always saying. You have three sentences, max,
all of them short, and they move in a pretty,
circular dance. Men are only men, you know,
front, side, back. There is nothing more to it. We
are all that is listed, in such fagging detail, on the
bottle – and nothing more. We cannot be blamed
for everything. Why don't you share what we
have, in a reasonable way? Here, take it. Take it,
woman! Is it infantilism, always to refuse? I heard
you use that word once, on some time-honoured
occasion, no doubt, with all the day's passing
celebrities gusting in – or out – out there in the
corridor, where the old boys used to sit – they may
still be there for all I know, Ronald and Gerald,
those two brave survivors, with all the others,
always a head taller than the rest, those two, such
a whiff of arrogance – so do check it out, as the
young tend to toss it out these days, check it out! –
those old boys, all twiddling their thumbs and
occasionally looking up. Without purpose. Well,

why not? It is always, always and forever nothing more than one thing after another, clippety clop goes the cart horse – slowly does it lest you bruise your heel on a carpet tack, goddamn it! The glances are long and without purpose. I feel for them. I am almost inclined to reach out. What stops me – other, I mean, than this great yawning gulf, which rather frightens me? Much like a menagerie on the make – if you can conceive of such a thing these days. I can. I do it all the time, left, right and then hands flat down on the floor as if it were a form of, a species of – I love that word, how forensically apt it always sounds – physical jerks. Which it is, of course, Frankly, how much can we expect of the brain these days, this mighty pulsing thing? A conference might address a thing like that, all proud old men, sitting tight, upright and alert, each one constipated as hell ha ha, sitting it out amongst the cobwebs, the drifting cobwebs from which, occasionally, they do swing like elderly acrobats.

It was in the morning, of that I have no doubt. I was waking up to it, this light. It was quite consuming me, to the bitter end, and perhaps even beyond. And would you like to know something? I mean it, really and truly. Not pretending. Not doing me a favour because I am still what I am, at least in part, you must understand. You did recognise me, I know, when you first saw me, you had no hesitation in recognising me, even whispering about me to a friend, and perhaps even pointing. You would, you would like to know! Say so then! Do say it! Do not hold back. And I for one would not wish to withhold it either. What would be the point when we have so little time? We need to show eagerness. We need to pullulate – what a jumping jack of a word! We need to go on and on. Who cares how tall the gate is, the one which leads into your father's field? Was it not? Am I wrong? Do tell me if I am – was it not just outside Saffron Walden, where you used to run like the wind? God, how I do remember that. I swear that if I forgot everything else, I would remember that because you looked so lovely. How many hundreds yards ahead of me were you? We can measure it, together, if we link hands. It is a matter of showing faith. Yes, I was glad just then. I was utterly glad with all the worldly gladness that I could ever muster, to be there, in that precious, almost otherworldly situation. Was it not everything that I had always been tending towards, that moment of such starkness, like the coy wink of a diamond on a finger end... Wait for it though. It must go on and on, spiralling on and on, until the conclusion perfectly satisfies all of us. Don't doubt me for a moment. I can pull it off. There is always a little additional space, that slight trick of buoyancy in the wings, and when perhaps you least expected it, when you thought that I had given my all and there was no more to give, that I had reached the point of perfect and utmost exhaustion... What then? Let me show you. You don't need to be shy of me. I want you to embrace me. You must embrace me. It will feel the right thing to do. The horses will rear up in front of us. Such mad, mad scamperings! Who said we could tame the horses? Who would ever wish to do it?

I have said it before, but you never seem to be listening. May is always the dearest month, always, a certain balminess, the promise of future good fortune, and even a horse shoe above the door. Who put it there then? Who remembers? Who knows to please me by reminding me in this way, so subtly, so profoundly so, of the virtues of May? I don't do it. And you are not even aware of my thinking because, as you tell me, it generally runs underground with little fear of emergence. And so let me now say it again, even if it means elbowing you aside rather rudely because, frankly, I have lost all patience: what happens in May seems to be a sort of paradigm for all the rest, a blessed interlude. Does that make any sense to you? Or will you merely go on patiently smoking, and leafing through your gardening magazines in the conservatory, with that nagging little radio voice just beyond the reach of audibility? You do disgust me from time to time. How I do love you though.

I call this latest move a tentative reach. The arm can only stretch so far. The bridges of Paris, many. The castles of Prague, horribly thronged these days. I gave a speech from *Cymbeline* once on that bridge, and someone threw a coin at me. When I went to speak to her, to thank her for her appreciation, I quickly came to understand that she knew not a word of English. I tried to ask her. I grew impatient. Why? Why? I said, pointing down to the coin in my hat. Had she thrown it down for a jest? She shrugged. She gave me the smallest kiss on the cheek imaginable. I would say that she was all of seventy-three – if a day. She was also a girl too, young, flighty. I knew! I could see through to it! That was the point of it. It was nothing to do with the money, which was, of course, derisory.

I made it all from string. It was all that I had to hand just then. You see, they gave me so little. They thought I would need nothing. How wrong they were. How wrong as usual. So I fiddled with it – arabesques in the air, one or two, and then a tentative lasso with which to hook the corner of the nursery chair. I liked that particular throw. It looked like proficiency. It looked like skill, pre-eminent, unsurpassed. It seemed to prove that I had been trained. Not so. I am an absolute beginner. Each day begins anew, with new legs, new hands, and even a slightly different voice. I have shucked of the Scots accent. Did you ever try one of those: sporran, kilt etc, all the kit for the roaming and the gloaming? Tedious. Ham-fisted. Type-cast. That's what they always said, the critics, those harumphing bumboys. That's what we always called them. You too. They dragged the words down from the topmost shelf of the dictionary, the day-before-yesterday's needless to say, dusted them off, ranged them in a certain utterly predictable order, and then, when it came to the next one, or even the one after that, they mixed them all up again, until you were left with a slightly different turn of phrase or nuance or perhaps a perfectly soluble mix of blame mixed with praise. That's all there was to it. I personally have set fire to twenty-seven critics in my time, all combusted in front of me, hair all red hot upward streaming, that's what I always tended to shout as it was happening – hair all red hot upward streaming! Even when they were as bald as coots and came hip-hoppitying along. Whoops, don't trip on your own inanities, boys and other random beastlies!

Is that what you asked? Did I hear you correctly? Am I tired? I am tired. Even to say so tires me because I know that you do not want to hear those words. Why would you? Your wish is to be magnetised, and even transported, by me. You do not want to stare, in a prolonged mood of tedium, at a collapsed sack of wind, a broken, hobbled chair, a deflated balloon, a damp squib, a hollow log, a magpie pierced through the throat with an arrow. This is the best I can do, for the time being at least. I am so sorry. I have turned out my pockets. Direct those dazzling lights, techie, on to my pockets in order to prove that I am not lying, that I am indeed spent to the uttermost! I have turned out my holes for you, my darlings. I have shown you the depth of my holes. And now you will just have to sit and wait – or leave immediately, demand a refund or some such. That way, there will be a little dribble of an evening remaining out there, beckoning you, perhaps in the direction of more productive diversions – bars perhaps, the turn of a milky thigh, raised up on a high stool on the swivel, the promise of a triple vodka shot or two to kill off your mind just in case you were inclined to stop thinking altogether. I would recommend that most of all. I would recommend an end to all torment because there is nothing worse than to be whipped along, dawn to dusk, like a moth-eaten donkey fit only for the knackers' yard. By the likes of me.

Should I stop? Would you like me to stop? Did you ever ask me to start in the first place? That is the point, is it not? You were never invited in the first place. You happened upon me, quite unexpectedly. The day had run its course, and then you blundered into me, and you must have seen some promise in me, I guess, or you would not have stayed this long. You would have vacated your seat in a trice, in a hurry. You would have not have paid good money to make any of this possible, and it has been made possible because you are helping to make it happen. So you are to blame for my being here, that is the truth of it. It is you who have conjured these words into being. Were it not for you, it would have been a different day altogether and I might, for all you know (and you could not possibly have known, could you?), have been perfectly silent, just imagine that. Just imagine listening to the pin drop. And you would have been someone else altogether. You would have been a person without me, with an intolerable sense of drift perhaps. I have pinioned you to your seat. We are a part of each other until memory fails us. You owe me thanks for that. Welcome, groundlings, to the company of each other. Clement weather? Or a thin, cold drizzle? May God help us to stick together.

It is as it is, you must understand. I chose nothing. I was chosen, let down gently at first, and then, a little later, in the reception room, our pride, with its ugly car-parking so clearly visible from the window, various altercations blew up, and from then on it was hell-for-leather towards the window, which opened out onto the embankment and all that roly-polying down that grassy slope towards the road, like kids, in our best gear. It was always yours, that side of the house, I seem to remember, you being of a naturally acquisitive nature. Gnash. Gnash. Gnash. That's how I always remember those teeth bearing down on me, from conversation to conversation. Until you were old enough to take them out altogether, or to replace them with something more gleaming. Glamour.

G for Glamour. You just flung out the word one evening as if anything could be credible, anything. Everyone free to choose. Complete mayhem in the kitchen. I did not like them, those dinner guests of yours, not one bit of it, more ape than human, far too much shouldering aside when one is trying to hold a paper plate in one's hand. What is the point of it? I ask you. Please. Pity me. Can you do any better – if you were to bother to try? Go on. Try then. Be my guest. We have all afternoon. They were not you at all. You could not address them either. They were like stupid, awkward children, always so many in this street or any other for that matter. Who invented children in the first place? They said no, no, no – it was such an ear-jangling chant – or turned their backs on us altogether in bloody-minded defiance.

I saw this figure of Love in the stream. It was a foul place, so polluted, cans, plastics, such like. And then, by way of a miraculous intervention – at least, that's how it seemed – this statue of love, life-size, and leaning over, concealing its face with its hand. It was so exquisite. I rather wanted to embrace it. Carrara marble, I would say. Shipped over. Or perhaps stolen from some museum and left here. I wanted it so badly. I rather wanted to embrace it. I wanted to find enough strength within myself to wrest it out of all that foul ooze, to give it back a life again. But it seemed perfectly contented there, half in, half out of the water. It did not speak. It did not move. Its gesture remained unchanged. I marvelled at its patience, that it could be in a mood of such serenity and benignity in north Sheffield of all places.

Yours for the taking. How could it be otherwise? We are only here once. A wisp. A breath. A single, out-flung arm. And then: nothing at all. Who walked away when I was speaking to you? She seemed not to hear (or perhaps not to heed), and yet what I was saying to you was meant for her too because I knew that it was perfectly useless telling you for a second time, when you had already once failed to hear me. And yet she too was walking away, she too was fiddling with her basket – rather in the way that you always did when you had forgotten something. We were all so privileged once. And what steps we took then, in the right direction!

Have I told you this? It was after you had fallen asleep. I was listening to your breathing. I made sure it was regular before I slipped away from you because I did not wish to interfere with your long, long beauty sleep. May it remain so now. That is what I would wish for you, for ever and a day, my darling. And this is what I did, you can read about it now. It is all done, all finished, the surface of the ocean is as smooth as we might ever wish it to be when we sit there facing it, and even dreaming a little for the sake of future good fortune. The day has at last returned to normal. There is no reason to feel nervous or challenged any longer. May your thudding heart slow now to a steady rhythm. Let me touch you also by way of reassurance. I chased away all the light on the stairs, to the last little shred of it. This is what I would wish you to know. It took me hours. It was playing games with me, fizzing up and then dying away, and then fizzing up again. It took me hours, and I succeeded, unaided. In time, in the fullness of time, I succeeded. Could you be said to be proud of me now, for having done what I have done? Could you? The microphone is switched off. Hold nothing back. We are all culpable.

You could say that it has always been the same,

life-long, facing down and then around. Easy. Once you get a good, firm grip on the handle. Favours, always too many favours back then. A little mistletoe too. No longer. Not any more, good soldier of ill fortune. Just call them sweeties then, popped into the mouth, one by one. Gob stoppers. So delicious. Always so delicious. You ramped up the occasion. You made it seem almost overwhelming. You saw a point to it all. There is never too much of this world for us, you know. It comes in stackings, heapings, entire warehouses full of the gods' golden opportunities, and all to be snatched away again by thieves who come in the night – creep! creep! creepy! creep! – ever so eager, always. Counting it all up, in these bags on the table, all that is left of me, after a fashion. You woke me then, rudely. You asked where, why, when, and I was far too sleepy to tell you. I was so far behind, and you were so far ahead of me. Do you think that I think in the way that you do? Am I expected to stand here in my stockinged feet and make sense of you once and for all? Spare me a moment. Let me at least breathe a little. Can you not grant me that? Must you forever be so importunate? And then the way you walked, always a little ahead of me, as if leading me on. I would turn away. I would step into the hedge, nifty as they go, and then wait, even sniff at the leaves for a moment. Rankly urinous leaves. Dogs have much to answer for. And yet I expected no less of you. Did it begin at that moment? Is that how, having both listened, heads pressed together, we are to describe it? Are we, for once – oh miracle! – in some kind of agreement? Let me hum tunes to myself, tunes, soothing, several of them, and all fond favourites. Take it away once again, maestro! I have plucked them all out of the air, one by one. I even took the liberty of scrambling two or three together. They were waiting. They were so eager to please me. They did not take exception to my behaviour, not for a single moment. On the contrary, they spoke of me to their gossipy friends, such as would listen, as if it were entirely normal, smooth-running, the optimum level of efficiency, I would say, had you asked me. Any factory is capable of achieving this kind of level of efficiency with the right attitude on the part of the men. Some are just cussed, and then you have to show a little patience, wait for the wind to blow over. And sometimes it seems to take forever. Forever! On the other hand – sorry to interject this little spoiler just as we are bowling along merrily enough, day after day, roaring along, two by two, hand in hand with the tooth fairy – most things are relatively normal if you stare at them long enough. You have to be so patient, always carrying the butterfly net in your napsack. Don't forget it, you little ninny and a half! Did I find that gratifying?

Did I even notice that you had done me such a favour, you, you, who did so few, and so intermittently, and especially when I craved a little goodness, the least intermission? We always loved that at the cinema, when the curtains slid shut so noiselessly, and we got back to whispering all that lovely nonsense of ours, yours more than mine because you were so inventive. You despised my inner cravings. You called me slut, harlot, wastrel, seemingly at random, which always amused me. It was never a part of you, to be with me when I conjured your presence amongst us. You had left, several times, and then returned in a great hurry. Of your choosing, of course. No one else counted. No one else took up the stick and beat the drum until it bled. Do you understand even a little of what I am telling you? I would say that you did not care. And yet that is not quite the case because you do manage to be present when I need you, which is seldom, because I have struck out on my own again today. Do you not see how the light is so exhilarating, directly up the fells, where we are walking so doggedly, and in the teeth of such driving rain? There were certain moments when I used to ask myself whether we would ever, ever arrive. Would we be stuck there, between the pine forest and the heather, with the light failing and the batteries in the torch going? It is a wonder, even now, after so long away, so long in ceaseless travel, that I have the heart and the strength to continue. And yet I do continue. It is within my nature to continue. I am a man of pluck and spirit, wouldn't you agree? No. Well then. That will not deter me. I have chosen a hat for the wearing. I have pulled on my boots. What more is there to be done or said? Well, there is all this laboursome explanation to set down in order that I shall be at one with myself, completely grounded. Otherwise, the world, once again, may go askew, flip over onto its back without warning, leaving us all stranded. And what use would that be to me? I may as well throw the fish back into the pond and be done with it, wave goodbye to all pond life, of which I am so overly fond. Always have been. A little like seeing you from behind in the mirror, how you turn so strange and so otherworldly when that happens. Your hump becomes exaggerated and even your voice, when you come to speak (seldom if ever), sounds a little more strangulated than might be customary.

A moment of triangulation, when the wheels move in sequence. The god's slow pace at such a time, in such a place, befits him, surely. Mine is not to stand here questioning when the air currents move in such a way. In that case, we can be said to be at one then. It is all so simple – like sliding across the floor, without hands. We have counted our beatitudes, of which there are many. Who now if not then? It is never a time to postpone the asking. All too urgent or pressing, or as you like. I lie here, oh dear, propped on my elbow, vaguely looking out, none too committed to this passing moment. In so far as your limb has withered on its stem, I deem you, to that extent, unfortunate. And you must surely agree – for once. Seldom, I am of course aware. Here it is then, what I had hesitated to say before now, before, in short, you interrupted me with all your nonsense. Sandpaper, when vigorously applied to the skin, is not bound to please. In fact, quite the opposite. This pole, which never fails to stride ahead of me, is a place for cogitation, at its highest point of rising, in the wilds, alone, without the wherewithal even to picnic daintily after all this serious climbing. What do you expect of me then, my friend? Something other than this? Am I to be some kind of a miracle worker? Not once, but several times, and always such gasps for breath. And then there is all this staring, this needlessly prolonged staring, but especially in Paris where they seem to wish to come at you with all teeth bared, and from all directions at once. I am always so inadequate in Paris. Every day tolls the passing bell, the call to do one's duty by death, and its prolonged and ever blacker aftermath. I am made to be much less of myself when in Paris. Run it past the teeth: Boulevard St Germain, Rue de Rochechouart. It sits on me. It spits me out. It vomits me forth. It farts me asunder. Who would be the least of these tiny glass splinters on a street of this kind?

Were you easily spoken to? Or is it better to be spoken of? Yes, these are the fists I shook. Embalmed now. In the local museum. Small enough to fit perfectly any boxing glove. Catch sight of them before all subsidies are withdrawn.

Tantamount to a death-knell? Did I hear you say that more than once? Would ears flap in the presence of a song bird? I am that song bird. Call me a house martin then. You are a poor, rackety, featherless thing by comparison. Set in a niche beside the road. Your feet are tied to the wire. You swing down and then round again, *perpetuum mobile*, in a sad, ever circling motion. Would there be any point in laughing at you now, when you seem so far removed from any serious exploitation or condemnation? Why have any truck with you at all? Because you are the voice which talks, that's why, you are the one who continues to expect answers, fully articulated and ridiculously long-winded, to all those ridiculous questions of yours, and I – more fool I! – I continue to provide them as if I had some duty to do so. How foolish could that be? Who gave me this role? And why have I chosen to star in it, year after year, as if it were profitable to do so, as if I even enjoyed it, as if someone were demanding it of me other than myself – and perhaps you, although I am not even sure of that anymore, not during all these tediously strung out afternoons of utterly futile whistling, because you spend so much time absenting yourself these days. Sometimes – from time to time – I wish that I had simply said no – as one sets one brick upon another when building a wall. Which is the sensible thing to do, always, with the watch on your wrist merrily ticking along, telling you the hour, when need be. As needs must from time to time. Not all higgledy piggledy. Not up, down and then around. Not forwards, backwards and then forwards again. Just the one word: no. It is so satisfying to slam a door really hard, causing the house to tremble to its very foundations, and then sigh in relief. Dust shaken off the feet, sweet Jesus. My oh my, what a romp we have made of it! Pardon? Excuse me? Did you just tumble out of a casket of gallimaufries? Or did I invent you for the sake of it? You tell me. You were always so bloody-minded when it came to learning the lines.

Seldom to be seen at all. Seriousness is out of the question. Not with any outcome in view. The terminus is here. Did you catch it? Was it all a little overwhelming – as you have been to me? Speak of the salad days, spill them all over the place. Spout much or little.

Yes. Yes. And yes again. A perfect fit. The eye and all that it sees, I mean. Puff-balls of mist are at last well settled across the terracotta roof tiles of the barn beyond and below this window, settling best where they dip, to create the shape of the wings of a bird in flight. That was our house once, was it not? In the Charente. We still have it. I even kept the tickets.

Perhaps an hour, and then gone. Could it have been so long? You said you were going to slip out. You made that here-and-then-gone gesture. Those were your words: slip out. Which rather suggests minutes (or even moments), not days, and certainly not years. Not here, now, without you. Certainly not that. Luckily you returned – quite speedily after my long sleep (was it?) – and I quickly pinned you to the wall with the aid of the old claw hammer! The age-old claw hammer. What a buffer! What a bruiser! What a well kept secret too for an otherwise quite unremarkable Thursday. I never wanted you to suffer.

Little by little we proceed, with hesitation, in all humility, apologetically. You, needless to say, strike out like a child with a drum, furiously beating. I should have kept you out there. They might have pinioned you to the floor, the brutes, the apes, the long-gones. Miss them? I do, strangely, and yet not at all. Not with so many tin tacks underfoot. So much more of a nuisance.

I speed you away from it all. It is in the air today, which is always so encouraging, little parcels of optimism to chew on. I take one in my hand, and I do the necessary. You are running now beside me, as we descend into the hole, and even there we both seek out and find, needless to say, illumination. I begin to talk to you again because there is no one to stop our conversation, no one to deny us this at-oneness in this hide-away place beneath the bed with all these books still gathering dust. Which I must clean because it is so bad for the health, you have always said. And I have not done it. I have merely added yet more books, almost as an act of defiance, though I do not regard it as such because I love you all so much, and this love will not go away as long as I think of it with care, and soothe it, and stroke it like a cat.

There are those who are blameless, needless to say. They strike out cleanly, across deserts, car parks, through sandstorms, all anointed, all set apart. Yes, the anointed ones. Iced in all purity like so many birthday cakes, jostling for attention on one small table top. No one hurries to join hands. They stink to high heaven. Wash off the impurities then. It is mete and right so to do.

The moments of blessing are few. We have all stepped aside, deftly, seeing nothing. None of this was within my gift.

I have asked your ghost for reassurance.
Tentatively granted, needless to say.

And then it was morning again, with puff balls of
mist well settled by dawn's light. I am dressed. I
greet myself. I express dismay with several audible
groans.

I have asked your ghost for reassurance.
Tentatively granted, needless to say. And then it
was morning again, and I was looking down over
the roof tiles, where the mist settles well, each to
his own precious prize. Puff balls? Or perhaps the
strange, translucent shimmer of icing. Let me bed
myself down here in all comfort. All-day comfort.
We hang from the roof tiles side-on. How to
fierce-grip? How to make a meal of it all without
food of any kind, up here, where the stars wing
down to graze on us? We are food for the stars, we
roof-clingers. All this is more than enough.

You, on the other hand, are here to be captured, known, acknowledged, affirmed, confirmed, but none of that deliberately set aside – unless you would set yourself aside. Open to question. Wide open. Is not the sky wide open? Was it not futile, and even laughable, that I should come with this tape measure hanging from my arm as if life, the world, the sky, my life or yours, were ever measurable? We dreamers are habitually known to bed down in tight-sealed boxes of such and such a dimension, of which I have just now ordered a score.

The light strikes glancingly, and then dissolves. No light. Some light. A little light, teeny-weeniest of lights, my listening boy-child. Or like a voice in a street. Any voice. Ask that it be empty of all content and, if not, why not. That sort of thing. Efficiency. Or a dice tossed down at random. The echoes of a distant footfall. A meaning set apart from us all, too indiscreet. It hovers, still. I catch at it. No truth is assured. No goodness abides. And then the morning sun across the tiles, mist well settled!

You were never present to thank me. I took it upon myself, in this chair, alone, obdurate, upright, and still seething with resentment as ever. No amount of gobbledygook frothing forth from the mouth would see us through. Nothing *is* to be seen through, ever. It is to be endured like the accidental burn from an iron. To the forearm needless to say. Or anywhere. Perhaps least of all here. And it is all so thin and so malleable, and I do thank them all. Wherever else if not here? There is only here. How could there not be? There is no question of dragging oneself away. Who would one drag anyway? And where? There *is* nowhere.

Caught in the act. Triply. At the furthest point from the trampoline – and for a man such as myself, the glad-handing liver of this breezy, no-holds-barred, posthumous life, to be nigh on up in the clouds again. Such exhilaration! With the aid of a bird's nest of wire conjured so speedily by you, who had not even been invited by such as myself. I alone was not on the list. And yet it was I alone who had contrived or compiled the list. Answer me that if the current mouth – mine, to be perfectly clear – will serve to see us through as far as yesterday, and then forever onward, I guess, unless your plan has changed it at all, which I doubt, very much.

Stab it. Stab it. Stab it? Where though? The heart, as far as we can ever be said to know it, is fully occupied in the downstairs bar, smooching around to the accompaniment of darkness, and a few impromptu, hole-in-corner, pianistic riddlings, needless to say. A holiday of sorts. For some – or many, if the crowds should happen to surge by. Unlikely. Choose, should you wish to measure my indifference. I do go there myself, on high days and holidays, but seldom accompanied by any measure of decency. What would I do were I obliged to drag another along? How would I cope? What in hell's name would I wear? Tell me, you fog horn you, down at the dock as the wherry approaches, slides in, like oil down the side of the glass, wheedling, worming its way. Would it be pig's swill to be voided from the stomach? Quite disgusting. Carry me away. Then bring me back smoothly, wholly contented with my lot. A lot. More than a footfall. More than a stagger with a mouthful of dribble. Able. Abel was I. Ere I saw Elba. Oh dear, another old trick from the box of fustian. When will they finally remember to seal the door to the attic of all our yesteryears?

Cobbles are to the foot or the mouth or the toe only so many, and frequently lost to view, and without discernible voice at all. Listen. Be attentive for a change. Try and see what I mean. And so we must *give* them a voice. It is all that is asked of us, and many do ask that much, so importunately too, as if it were all a matter of too much urgency. And everywhere, you know, urgency is afoot. Nothing to stop the blood flowing unless you staunch it. And I do – *when* I do, that is, and not every day is a day such as today, with the intricacy of its winding stairs going up and up and up, and how I look at you, always, almost as if you were not really there at all, and it was I who were uttering the words for the two of us, only for the two of us. And is that not more than enough? No, no, there can never be too much because, you may have noticed, there is always too much of it already, between the sweat and the dirt and the grease of these sheets for example, or swept across the tiles like the hurried wheeling and massing of swallows, forever oncoming when we least want or demand or expect it. Who would be condemned to be such as they? Who would choose to whistle blithely like a bird? I need rest. I cannot go on like this. There is always too little breath for the too many words to be uttered, and on and on they go, enough to make you weep in exhaustion. I shall give up soon. I shall give myself up soon. Unless you let my words drop with the sobering clunk of metal.

God speed, she said, almost beneath her breath, as if it were a secret to be kept. And who needs secrets when we have heaven, always, above and beneath us, this all-encompassing heaven of love and sanctity, were it not, of course, for this dreariness all over too, like endless wallpaper paste... More than a tad disappointing, even to myself were you ever listening, and I doubt it. Yes, you truly disappoint me. You deserve to be stripped of yourself at the stroke of a pen. Do I not at least deserve your full attention, catastrophe or not? Have you not paid good money?

Morning again, and never rid of it, the nuisance of its bright-eyed look, so demanding, so daily. I will have none of it. Let me sweep it from this room as one sweeps away so many puff balls of dust, and always so vigorously. The idling of the hours again. What I cannot so much as abide is the cheek of it all, your cheek, dainty though you were when I first caught sight of you. Glancing by me like a small and quite refreshing breeze, bobbing or even spinning, like a pink plastic toy, one of several, attached to the front of a pram for a child to dandle and gurgle by. Such tidal onrushings of loveliness, never to be repeated until, quite simply, at the moment of their tuneful arrival, I lost them again, being the habitual humbuggery that I am. And then you fell in, head-first, and there was no one nearby, not a worm or a slug even, to pull you out. I climbed down, all the way down, that long metal ladder into the dank and overwhelming dark, and there I looked about for you, and you were nowhere. You were palpably nowhere, quite overwhelmingly absent. Only your words were smeared across the walls, smeary dashes and daubings of your words so easily recognisable as yours. Had you, of all honourable people, been reduced, in time, to graffiti? Is this all that the cruelty of a harsh and forever-onward-hurrying world had seen fit to make of you? And then there were all those corridors, and rooms leading off into other rooms, and it was all so hopeless, and I was always so helpless, now as then, groping, fingering the air as if the air were substantial enough to be fingered, which it was not, even I knew that. Why could I not stop myself then? Why did I not snatch up a book from the shelf and talk some sense back into myself, measure the day in all its unavoidable, unputdownable atmosphere of happy homecoming? And yet my good sense could not prevail, in the end, against all this nonsense. There was always too much of it. And so I withdrew to my bed again, ten o'clock at night, the habitual hour of my retirement, by which time I have always had more than enough of it all, and more than enough of myself into the bargain, I scarcely need to add. I feel wholly glutted with myself, disgusting, ever oncoming. There are too few opportunities to hand it all back. There ought to be entire weeks and months of happy, queueing men, bent over and reeking in their mothballed overcoats, and I amongst them, one undistinguishable from another. Take me back to the sea again, I say, calling out for the usual sympathetic response never yet once granted, where I can sprawl on my back, and be lifted and then lowered again, sometimes quite gently, and at other times not. It all so much depends upon the weather on that coast. So cold and so unpredictable, the North Sea. When the sea speaks, it does so in a roaring, carousing, sailory voice, quite laughable really, though I seldom laugh because the truth is that it terrifies me, any oncoming, upsurging body of water can terrify me. The voices are those of drowned men, with so few reasons to be happily nudging the barnacles.

Yes. Yes. Yes. Hammer them in like nails driven into a wall. Bang, Bang. Bang. Such exhilaration when the arm moves to a rhythmical tune such as this one: bang, bang, bang. I feel like a child entire again. The years have rolled off me like grease from the inner walls of a rusted drum. I spring up like any tough-stemmed plant sipping at the sweetness of the circumambient air. Whose life is this anyway? Surely not mine! This is what words are for then, I tell myself (as so many times before), to be hammered in so that they remain fixed and dependably, reassuringly close when all else is waveringly distant and slippery as shifting sands are undependable, or when mud sucks at the foot and you can scarcely drag out half of a leg, let alone the foot on the end.

The tray spins through the upper air, and I go to catch at the tea cup and the saucer, one and then another caught quite easily, and then settled down in my lap here. And I sip at my tea, and it is a murky, sludgy brown to look at, and it slips down so easily. Where the dead do not swim, across the surface of the tea, in steady circular motions, heedless of my protestations. And yet I said not, not. Why then do they swim at all when I have said not, when I have expressly forbidden it because the tea tastes quite disgusting mingled with the limbs of the dead, and I am of course aware that they are dead in spite of the swimming motions? Swimming is the kind of base treachery to which I can scarcely apply my mind. Or perhaps it is merely illusory. One or the other. The tea has settled back. I am contented. Little is needed. Merely to sweep away the dead with a long-handled broom.

Those castles in the air are made of sand, and no sooner do I build them than they trickle back to earth in sweet defiance of their maker. And so I build them again, occupying exactly the same cone-shaped air spaces, just above brow height, so that they are well within reach of my rising and falling arms, scooping sand from the bucket with my fingers, and then lifting, lifting it. General sweetness, like cubes of sugar, one after another, held on the tongue as they dissolve, little by little, and all that sweetness slips down the throat. Sugar and sand, oh happiest of bedfellows.

It was not much to ask of myself, and so I made the proposal, and then I stood back, and I waited for the response. It was a request to drive the hand along, this hand which grips the pen, the left, hour after hour, every live-long day, for the first three hours of the day, in order to discover what exactly it might consist of, everything that would emerge from such enforced labour. Would there be bees? Would there be showers of rain? Would there be much seemingly casual conversation? Or would it merely consist of unanswered and unanswerable questions, asked over a tedium of hours, questions so burdensome, questions so tiresome, questions so ridiculous, questions so unfathomable? Who would insert them? Who would have the courage, the gall, to make that first incision? From what dark depths would they have been dredged? Certainly the terrain was well wooded, there would be no problem about that, with sun-dappled clearings in which to sit with the picnic basket, the bread, the wine, the cheese, and much pleasingly desultory, sun-dappled – yes? – conversation. Who would not wish for such conversation – were it announced in good time. No point at all in describing it after the event, when the woodland was felled, and the city fully established, and the names of the speakers barely even recognisable on the tomb stones at the extreme outer edge of the abandoned quarry. Why induce depression? Who in his right mind would go for that? Who would even want to hear of it? Who would subscribe to it? None of us, we all chorused in unison or uniform as we slunk back to the partial and intermittent relief of so much shallow, tepid water.

And yet I do wish to establish all this, once and for all. Otherwise, what exactly is the point of it? Why am I standing here asking this question? Why am I writing these words if you lack the appetite, you tell me, to read them? And why do I lie down here at nights, so close to you, and sleep the sleep of the unsound? Why would I crave your attention if I did not think that in the end you would judge it to have been worth it? There is no such thing as blahdiblah. There is no world in which blahdiblah could be said to exist for any man with his life trotting briskly ahead of him. Unless I am wrong, of course. Unless it exists in this world, and I am its inventor. I cannot assure you of that fact. You must tell me whether or not you believe it to be true. I remain wholly sceptical – as if before an un-carved joint of meat on the kitchen table. We lack for a knife with a keenly sharpened blade. We lack for words of praise. We even lack for plates, a table, a table cloth, a room in which to contain it, a roof pendent to safeguard the guests from unappetising squalls of rain. What we do not lack for is mouths, drooling spittle, the appetite to continue in a heady mood of ravenous delight – this far at least. Contentment enough for a single small box then. More than enough until midnight at the very least.

This far at least? Did I say? Did it say itself? Has it taken control? Is that my fear? That there is nothing here but that which turns up so rudely and without even so much as an invitation? Every word, you must understand, has been invited. Nothing has slipped in without my noticing. There were so many to choose from, so many who might have wished to join us here, at this telling. And I turned the great majority away because of shape, weight or general attitude. I have no appetite for bullying or disobedience. Our world, this world of our making, must be honed to perfection. We must all pull our weight, intolerable though it may prove in the end to be.

The sheep swelled up one by one. I did nothing. It was not of my doing. I merely stood there and marvelled as each one ballooned in his or her turn, sheep, rams, lambs, all patiently waiting in line to swell and then, having faltered for a moment on their tippety toes, rise up into the air above the meadow. And when they had risen, and were comfortably settled on their invisible shelves of cloud-padding in the upper air – there were seventy of them in all, old and young, I counted – they gently nudged against each other to the accompaniment of the most touching of bleatings and baahings, as if they were so grateful to be up there, risen so far above all earthly care.

I struck it all out, at once, with a gesture of uncustomary violence, because none of it was at all seemly. Would you call that foolishness – or an uncustomary display of strength of character? And, if so, why, at that precise moment, did you crane your neck like a goose? Mockery. I have done enough with mockery. I have seen enough for one lifetime. I created an entire playlet of the stuff – in my days of playleting, so long gone, so muchly many – and I remember even now how it unfolded, so smoothly, down the tiles as if it were so much mist, sweet to the eye as sugar candy, rolling out like an unruly blanket, spreading on all sides, yes down the tiles of the roof, the terracotta roof tiles, their thickness then when held in the hand, as mist always used to roll, and I would look up then to embrace it as it came on towards me, and even as I reached out with my arms to welcome it, it would disperse again, like a wronged lover, a coy temptress of anyone's everyday dream of seduction, of which there have been so many – dreams, that is. I have always let you lie because you never wanted to be disturbed. I would think to rouse you at all hours of the day or night, in those places where you would be sleeping - birds' nests or the crevices of rocks, so high and so wind-bitten, and I would find myself climbing towards you in all my headlong eagerness to share my life with you, and you would always be sleeping. Quite deliberately, I have no doubt of it, because, oh just moments before, you would have been clambering, scrabbling, on all fours, up the hill-side in the company of all our sheep and our goats, singing along with them, always so playfully, in all the overflowing abundance of your youthfulness. And it is that I would yearn to capture, the bottled spirit, sealed and bottled for immediate consumption, of your youthfulness, so mountain-fresh, so fragrant, so elegant. And then, at last, I would snap. I would raise you up and shake you about, quite roughly, in order, at last, to discover exactly what there was of you, what remained of you after all these years of long waiting and silence and frustration. Would you yield yourself up to me at last? You were a sealed tin, battered and bruised, but nonetheless sealed, always sealed against me.

Flinging myself about in the entrance. And then smartening myself up again – collar, buttons fastened, one by one, to the topmost strangulating one. It was the only way. It was the method I had always chosen for pulling the body back into shape. At nights it would fall away into such spilling, disgusting shapelessness, the way the stomach would wash sideways, oozing forth in all its fleshy pallor, across the bed, as if it were a sheet of fatty scum, skimmed off a polluted river. Much too disgusting even to consider. As a sweet alternative, on the other hand, there is the notion of life's being always lighter than it used to be, and how it skips now along, a phantom seeking out the best of itself as it goes, never too quick or too deft for its own happiness, with the capacity to leap over hills and then down again into enshadowed coombs, where it will lie hidden for hours at a time, and then leap up again, as if nothing has happened at all, and nothing it ever does is at all surprising – nor ever will be. And yet life must be a surprise, perpetually, or what good would it do to live it if you knew of what it would consist, second by second, even before it came on? Life must strike out at you like a glancing blow to the side of the head, sending you reeling, in all its headlong unexpectedness.

The clods are piled up, one upon one, against the side of the house, as if in preparation for... No one has ever told me what is to come, for what we may or may not be preparing ourselves, why the things of this world are as they are, both maddeningly haphazard and also quite otherwise, prinked into groups and mounds and small, orderly convocations. I have asked and asked, of everyone, passers by in the street for example, accosting them, one by one, for the answer to each new day's enigma. I have said to each one: look at this sky now, and how it sweeps blandly across, as if combed by wisps of cloud drift, seemingly without comment, as if it has nothing to share with us – or has no wish to share, which is surely much worse, that degree of ingratitude. Nothing. A thunderous nothing comes, by way of response, and even a disgusted turning away, a sharp presentation of the raised shoulder, as if my question has poisoned the very air we might all wish to breathe. And then I have said to myself: what exactly is in the nature of a look? I have asked myself again and again, what does it all amount to when the mouth will not open, when it remains so thin and so tight-sealed as this? I have even reached out with my fingers, and endeavoured to part the lips, to facilitate the passage of air, which might itself then facilitate the passage, the quick onward gush (one can forever hope) of words. What good are words which do not flow readily, which hesitate, halt, die away into silence, even before they arrive? My own flow, torrential, and always within, resembles, and perhaps even deliberately mimics, the troubled movements of the inner body, in the churnings and the gurglings of its night hours, that is how my words go, like a great underground stream flowing, washing back and forth, each one clashing with others, or entire sentences in confrontation with each other, questions asked, questions deftly parried, questions unanswered, strange wheedling half-responses, random ejaculations.

You are not mine to deny me. And I am not yours to deny you. And so – it comes to us all in the end – there is this necessary separation, this rough tearing apart, which causes, in time, infinite howls of pain of every kind, which may include street noises, and even the crash of a car against a wall, when the body slumps forward and bleeds from the mouth, and we go to rush across. And yet we are not even there. We are not those witnesses. There is no car, and no body. There are merely these screechings of pain, like a knife blade across a sink, and they have emanated from within. Is that sufficient reason to faint?

We have made it all back to the opening, to this aperture, which is so much smaller than anyone had ever promised. Of a finger's width. A child finger's width. But who has an eager child to hand to do such a thing? Are their voices not behind that indomitably tall school wall, all merrily shrieking at the tops of their innocent voices? Is loneliness then a game? Does it not all – and must it not always – amount to this: to a certain dodging and weaving between the houses until no one can be said to see you because all life, all the breath and the bounce of it, has been so skilfully avoided? The comfort of a passing stranger consists of nothing but this in the end. The stranger is nothing but an image in the mirror, so dependably unrecognisable.

Godliness does happen. It arrives at a wall, point blank, so tense and so accusatory, and then it swerves off to the left when commanded by any passing voice, cloud-conjured. And this is more than enough for contentment, all these tiny instances of god's pillow talk, when he passes to you a swift suck of the juice of comfort in the desert of the bed in the early morning. You have reached out, expecting nothing, and there has been something. And something, every least little something, is always more than enough. By way of a warning, you must understand. Your life is not inclined to overspread itself. All these old blankets, as usual, are moth-riddled.

Keep the last for us, remember. And then hold it all together. Do not betray us. Be steadfast. There is nothing worse than random spillage, across clothes, floors, pavement. No one was ever invited. They became the intruders. We sanctified them in that way, we made them special. Outcast turned intimate at a stroke...of their own newly minted good fortune. What more should we ask of ourselves on a June morning, at such a moment of expectation, when the spade hangs idle, and the camera has been set aside, unwanted? And let no one know what has happened. Perhaps we should say – let us practise it all together – that it did not happen. Time has been set in reverse. We are soon to live in the nineteenth century. We are packed in preparation. We have learnt the walk, the poise, the gravity. We have bitten down on the coinage, and we have not found it wanting.

Did the women happen though, without adequate warning? Did we make them happen or did they arise and then just as quickly fade away again of their own accord? Do we care that this hand in mine, so pulpy and so yielding soft, is a dead one, and that it could not be otherwise? We have walked in parallel for far too long. We have not learnt to divagate, meander, make small-talk, say nothing at all. Would you say that that was the least of our problems? Or are you beyond all saying now, being so monumental? I walk around you at least three times every day. More than quite sufficient, I would say. Is the pigeon shit a-calling? Is there still a mast over there to swing from? I would say not, though there are many here always so ready to contradict me, and I do understand that, the spirit of contradiction, because we are always so raring to go, always. There is this life, and it is hot in the hand like a chestnut fresh out of the oven, to be tossed, with a happy yelp, from hand to hand. We play with it. We defy it. We run it on ahead of ourselves and then, little by little, a bit later on, we begin to draw it back and to examine it more minutely, as if it were a precious thing all along and not some fly-by-night, flibbertigibbet sort of a thing.

Who has done this to me? Who has had the gall, the wit, the brazen cunning, the temerity? These garments have never been so shivery loose about my body. They remove themselves without appeal. I stand by, helpless, arms raised, arms slumped down. I never know what hour of the day it may come to be – or whether it will come at all – because light alternates with dark now at such speed, flickering on and then off again, the light, the dark, the light, and so on. And my age too is so driftingly permeable. I see through to the lispings, the headlong tottery steps, of childhood. And then, having blinked in consternation, my bony fists are beating on the roof of the coffin, which sways along alarmingly to its final resting place, to the accompaniment of a steady drone of low voices, not one recognisable. Have I ever been truly alive? And, by way of recompense for all this spasmodic torment, may I now request – of he or she or it or them – to be alive again? At your convenience. Do not part the truculent waves for me alone.

Yes, this is the place. I recognise it at last. My eye admires the angle of the hillside. I peer down into the threatening dark of the chimney. I watch that white dog I once knew, still turning and turning in its sleep. It is all running ahead of me today, and I lie here wheezing, trying to still or to slow down my breath. Will I ever catch up, make amends, seize hold of every passing moment again? Nothing is as it was. All has turned a smeary yellow. The clouds are not in their places. I have lost the capacity to see far. There is no farness to see. It is all backward-looking, as if my body were moving in reverse, back down the long years to the nothingness of the womb. Will I be safe there? Will there be expectancy, a certain apprehensive cheerfulness? It catches at me now, and then again, snags, pulls back on me. You are tugging at my sleeve. Leave me alone. Let me make my way without complaint or questioning. What, after all, is there to say? That we sat there once at a small, round table, and grimaced towards the window as you raised a cup and then drank, eyes averted, barely noticing me? Could that be enough by way of an accounting for it all, little bits and pieces of that kind? Will they be sufficient? Were there not matters of great moment then? Did it all merely dribble along inconsequentially, day by day, unheeded? Was there so little of it then, laughably so? And were our movements, passing to and fro along street or corridor or... Yes, you see how I falter. I hesitate to pull it round in the direction of a conclusion because there is so little and so much to be said, and all so intractable. The past, I guess I mean – whose guess though, and why now? – and all the sloppy, formless guilt of it.

Next to the others, all of them, singly and in large gatherings, pushing and jostling, bad-mouthings and slap-downs, by the playhouse or in a street, milling and talking, heads bobbing like those Italians in that public square at Bologna – such fierce debate amongst themselves! So much to be unravelled! So much to be contested! And such hats! And such inform greyness! I am always amongst them, head raised high like a bird, willing myself to be a glad participant. And yet I never was. All would fall away. I would burrow, deeper and deeper. I would walk away, shrugging my shoulders. What am I here? What are they there?

Is this not yet another example of the overwhelming littleness of it all, how it all dices away into fragments ever smaller and smaller?

For the first few miles, must I carry the tiles on my back? There was no other way. When I asked how, they had shrugged their shoulders and then pointed, perfectly nonchalantly, to the heap of tiles. I had ordered roof tiles, terracotta roof tiles, for the barn within clear view of our window, that window which opened out like a door onto the upper air, as if willing us to leap forth... I looked down and across into the valley, where the mist always settled of a morning. I loved that mist. It enveloped me. It was as much a bed of comfort as my own poor bed. And there it settled, amongst the roof tiles. How had it all been made whole again? I looked. I wondered. I looked again. In a wheelbarrow? How had they arrived? Were there ladders, ropes, hods, men? Surely I had not been equal to the task. There must have been others! And now there is no one to tell me. They have all gone from here, with their filthy hands. Between my determination to buy them, and my sight of them there, all healed and harmonious in their sweet, sun-blessed regularity, below the window, just a little below the level of my eye, there is a great gulf of memory. It is like some trick seen by a boggle-eyed child on a stage, amongst all the colourful collapsible boxes, and the tall hats, and the conjuror's wand, and the disappearing and newly reappearing rabbit, and the winking and smiling rotund little man who must surely be the conjuror himself, how I think of that leap from one to the other, those tiles heaped high in the yard, cupped in a towering heap, one inside another, and their appearance, in perfect formation, on that roof. It as if I had conjured it all in order that my comfort here in this attic room should be complete. And it is complete. It is all true. My tiles, the gleam of them there, when they are mist-coddled or rain-sluiced, they make for a wholeness of the soul, a careful, kindly knitting of the disparate parts, a great coming together so that we all know who we are and how and where we belong in this otherwise world of utmost boredom and futility and lassitude and hopelessness and helplessness. The tiles bring me together. They make me as one with it all. They seal me. They bond me. They affirm my at-oneness with myself. They make the heavens bow down to the earth in homage, and the waters coyly kiss the land.

Within sight of so little. The catalpa tree, she with

her leaves of such a beauteous, translucent, summery sheen, has turned her back on me, and now faces down towards the lane. She no longer sings her full-voiced hallelujahs of song at me. She is in a mood of high dudgeon. The rain disfigures the slates just beyond the door, making them shine with a dark and slippery menace. There are no railings any more, and so it would be a matter of plunging head-first onto the gravel. Cuts. Bruises. Shockings beyond measure. Even the lavender cowers, leans away as if shrinking from me, wind-whipped, beside the gate. Where you went, I still see. But it is almost, and also – note this now – as if I see beyond. There is a flame-like trickle of path in the middle air where you still walk. It is as if a flaming red pencil has been smudging its way along in front of me, seconds in front of me, because you are never far ahead, and that is your charm, that you are never far distant from me. It is as if the moment that you left – I could hear you rattle-yanking open the door – I leaped out of bed and ran down the stairs, two by two, in pursuit of you, so shocked and delighted to have heard your returning footsteps, that customary impatience as you worked with the key to release yourself – it was always such a botheration to you, working with that key in that door – and then, having done so, slammed it, hard, after you, as if to make plain to me what you were doing, that you were escaping from me again! Did I dress? Did I have time for such nonsense? Clothed or not, I see myself, even now, standing at the door, panting, ready to be gone, ready to run in pursuit of you. But just as I arrived there, in the moment of my standing there and looking out at the filthy weather, a great sobering seized hold of me. You had left me entirely. The flame was snuffed out, utterly consumed. There were no smudgings of redness lingering on in the air. A terrible shivering grabbed hold of my body until my teeth rattled in my head and I heard myself howling in misery.

Is this the moment to ask? It is the moment to be interrogated. Once and then again. A slow reprisal perhaps. A slow beginning again, and then once again, and then forever once again. Who was it spoke just then? You? Or some other like you, even a little like you? Or some other unlike you, whom I have foolishly mistaken for you? Must I carry on? Well then. Is it walking that will see you through? Those who do not walk dissolve back into nothingness, first inserting themselves, neatly, into small glass jars, holding their breath, barely believing it possible until it is well and truly done and dusted. You are out there, on the outside, looking in at at me, and even tap-tapping on the glass to gain my attention. My sleep is so much feigning, let me tell you that now because everything needs to be told in the end, all rooms to be swept clean of worldly pother in the end. You were tapping, and I was looking, and yet my eyes were closed against you, and I could see through my closed lids. In fact, my seeing was more acute than it had ever been. I could see you. I could see through to our beating heart. I could watch your lungs working. I could see through your head to the mantelpiece at the back of the room where our pictures stood propped and waiting, pictures of just the two of us, arm in arm, looking like twin ghosts, twin abominations. You were speaking to me, but no words reached me because the jar was so thick, and so heavy-lidded. It was, I believe, a pickle jar, long in my keeping, which would explain why it reeked so of fish, why I found myself gagging on the reek of fish, which distracted me so from your words because I know that I could have made them out, I could have understood you, I could have been embraced by you in so many words, had I paid attention to the exaggeratedly slow movement of your lips. Because you were trying. For once in your life you were trying. You were, quite deliberately, reaching across to me, giving me all your love and attention, as if every word and every last gesture were meant, to the uttermost. Your eyes had never been so imploring, your mouth never so winningly close and moist and red and warm. And there was I, thin as a twig, awkwardly coiled, marooned, in a jar. Who had put me there? I knew the answer to that question. I had no need to ask. Such foolishness to put such a question to myself! I knew that it was I who had put myself there. They had asked for volunteers, and I had stepped forward without a second's hesitation. I had wanted to be there. I had wanted the security, the solidity of life in a jar at last. All my life I had wanted it, yearned for it. I had walked up and down the corridors of supermarkets, day after day, week after week, month after month, and I had yearned to be a pickle, a pepper, anything still and assured and poised and certain, a thing waiting to be chosen, and a thing which would indeed be chosen by someone in the end because it would be so desirable. I knew that, were I to present myself in that way, in a jar, at some point in the future of my errant life I would be violently plucked out between finger and thumb (or upon the thin tine of a silver fork), and be admired by the eye for long on long and then, finally, savoured to the utmost. As was happening now, of course. You were savouring me so. Your eyes were draining me to the dregs.

And yet I could not hear our words. I could not see your lips because my mind was so completely distracted by that reek of stale fish. It was as if I were that fish, that stench of dead fish, myself, that, having aspired to be a proud thing in a jar, I had made the fundamental error of choosing, from all jars available to me on the shelf – and there were always so many empty jars on the shelf – I should have chosen the jar which would prove to be a curse to me, which would somehow interpose itself between us, so jarringly, at this shared moment of such overwhelming sweetness, which would say no, no, no to me, to us.

Seen to be lifted off and up. One. And then another. And then stacked in high, teetering heaps, and carried away so uncertainly. Or peeled away in two or threes, at a certain speed, from the table (old and mahogany, surely), with such acknowledged dexterity. Knowledge, book knowledge, lifted up like that as if such out-loud-speaking knowledge were transportable from place to place in blunt, fat objects such as books, quite heavy, quite clumsily heavy, when you blundered against a wall and spilled them all onto the floor, and they landed spread-eagled, words, words, words painfully smacking the floor, face down, and inwardly bruised if not bleeding. Could a book bleed? Did single words – what of 'heart', for example? – bleed? Certainly. If taken amiss. If misunderstood. If wilfully misinterpreted by the careless, the idle, the brutish. Or if dropped to the floor. My job then was to stand in the midst of the readers, the seekers, the shelf gropers, anticipate when a book might be harmed, and then run to its aid, making a sideways leap, for example, when I saw one falling from a careless hand, or position myself, fully stretched – arms spread, legs straight out just as far as they could be urged to go – on the floor so that when the entire stack spilled in a slow and terrible arc from the librarian's frail and trembling arms, I would be there to catch each one, reaching out, to left or right, with my hands, or projecting a foot to guide one to a gentler tumble upon a stretch of carpeting. Anything that might prove necessary to prevent the death or the serious maiming of any single book, such was my task, my vocation, my dream of myself, yet to be realised, it has to be said, even as I stare at the mouldering, sorry specimens which still remain within my proud ownership.

I was not the first to acknowledge the truth of falling. Others had seen it. Others had suffered. Even humans. Even bricks from a wall. It is tiredness which makes it so. A house tires, falls to its knees. A dog wearies of living, turns in a circle on its stinking mat, gives up the ghost. A tray knows when its time has come – delicate cups shatter, spoons jostle in confusion and disfavour at the foot of the stairs. Every day I have fallen inside myself. It is not the body's fall which is most to be feared, you see. A body's fall is nothing – who cares for a broken bone or two? A bone can be mended with sticky tape and spit and glue and a flung out promise. It is the spirit falling away from itself, the spirit which finds itself the victim of the most terrible lassitude. It is in that moment of waking, when you have lost yourself, all compulsion to be and to think and to see and to do have gone, in a single out-breath, as if it were some evil conjuring trick. Some thief in the night has crept in and stolen you away from you. You no longer remember your name. You no longer remember your purpose, your direction of flight. You no longer remember what it is to make that slow, gentle arc of a piss into a bowl. You hover there over, swaying a little, mind fogged, leaking at random here and there, weeping a little too, utterly uncomprehending, fingers wet to the touch. Should you return whence you came? But where had you begun? You look back through the murk of dawn to see a flight of stairs wavering a little in front of you, a door to its right. You reach out with your hand, but your hand freezes, dead as a wooden strut, even as it projects into the air. It freezes in salutation. But who are you greeting? With whom are you pleading for the return of sense, vision, clarification? There is no one there. All life is sleeping. All life has slipped away. All life is elsewhere. Will you ever recall again how it once teemed and teemed?

And then there was, always, all that mad-cap running, everywhere, down and across and up and back, to the shops for mother, to the doctor, to the hospital where all the tedious waiting would take place, after all running was ended, during that posthumous life I am still living. My legs are pulsing. I feel the inside of them, still, forever agitating to be away, away. Something drums there, frantically, when my mind's eye catches sight of a rising field, a track across it, sinuous and beckoning. I go. I am gone. I am here, still. They threw me about, roughly, and then they left me. There had been a conversation, some high carousing notes, as if in the middle of a drinking bout to which I had not been invited because I was lying about my age, and they were standing over me, leaning, deep-peering at me as if I were a specimen of the utmost fascination. This is what I am then: a specimen to be poked at. Little by little they disassemble me. I try to explain in my new small voice that this is not what it is to be, this is not my bodily's purpose, to be dismembered in this way, as if I consist of so many foolish, futile, ugly, ungainly parts. I try to sketch out for them the whole that I have always been, but some part of them looks right through me, sees beyond me to a fuller vision, which is no doubt *their* vision, of my future, which is no future at all because I am no longer the participant. I will no longer speak for myself because a toe, a knee, a liver, has no voice of its own. It is a helpless nothing to be flung or given away. That is all they know of me now: these bits of pieces they are so eager to examine, pick apart, hold up to the light. In short, I am to be donated because I am a nothing to be reckoned with. I am a nothing.

In the interim, let us all breathe a little. There are so many places and such opportunities. You were there again, and I touched you. Or I thought to touch you. Or I dreamt of touching you. You were not mine – just as I am not mine. How could that happen anyway? The world's makeweight of unfathomable questions. We are all so carefully set apart, tweezered into these old tobacco tins in which we habitually kept all the nails and the screws of various sizes and, indeed, all the whatnots. Always so useful, that great, teetering tower, and so monstrous in its overleaningness. There were backs and fronts, and to the side there were the darkened rooms or alcoves in which all the whispering took place, and I would eavesdrop there, unwanted. I would be shooed away by a flurry of naked limbs. Did you ever have an inkling of what I was up to? And even before I met you? Would that have been possible, do you think, that the thought of a thought can precede another thought? I have always thought so. I have even been emboldened by such assurances, daily, nightly. The bell has tinkled for me – somewhat effeminate, it has to be said – and I have come running, breathless and ever so eager. Always so eager until now, until this fit of inertia. I have screeched to a halt. I was going, hell-for-leather, and then the car swung in a slow arc across the slippery surface – was it? – of the road, lost control, and wedged itself side-on to the oncoming traffic. And there was such a general commotion, such a pile-up! I could scarcely breathe at the thought of it. It was as if someone powerful had seized me by the throat, caught hold of my windpipe and squeezed me with such violence that I fell unconscious. I spun-rolled away from myself, into a gully of sorts, a rainwater gully, where an abundance of sweet, cold wetness soused me, washed over me again and again and again like so many waves spilling over me on the seashore. Where? What? Who? some part of me was continuing to ask: Where? What? Who? And who was adequate to frame a response to such questions? There were none qualified thereabouts. They were all hoodlums, make-weights, shifty nonentities, street-corner beer-swillers, oddballs. None upright. None possessing one iota of charity or clarity of purpose. In short, no one to cling to. As a man might cling to a buoy. And I was that boy, needless to say, albeit a specimen far too aged for the distant harbour lights, bless them to high heaven...

Oh you have said it then! We took a vow not to speak, and you broke into the silence without a single word of apology. I didn't know what to do. Should I rise up? Should I lie flat again? Should I conjure new worlds of promise to replace the old and tired redactions?

Is it you? I asked. Because you had left again the very second you spoke – as you would always do. You never stayed to judge the consequences of your actions, you always left me there, in the middle of the floor, bent over, scrabbling at the fragments with my fingers, those many, many thousands of broken egg shells. Is there anything more makeshift, would you say? If you were ever inclined to speak again?

I had never wanted to tell you this. I had waited for the moment. Where there is ink on the fingers, there is always a haunting. There is the haunting of words not quite formed, words preparing to fling themselves at you without mercy. No amount of scrubbing at the hands will do. There is no cleansing. There is no absolution. There is no final forgiveness. You are always at the mercy of that which will be given to you. The abiding stain of the unanticipated word, the word you meet, quite by chance, at the table in the corner of the cafe, written down perhaps on a scrap of paper left there by a stranger who is evidently not a stranger because he knows you and understands you, through and through, birth to death and all points in between... That word, once raised, once read, even idlingly, nonchalantly glanced at, will bring about a general conflagration, a deluge of aftermaths because that single word will be linked up to other words like prisoners in a chain gang. They are there already, waiting to spill forth, in all their keen and accusatory orderliness, and always unglimpsed until that morning's seemingly casual moment in the café. You had judged the day to be a peaceful one. And how wrong you were. Now everything has to be rearranged, from foot stools to horizon line. It is likely to keep you busy for a lifetime of days.

Was it not like that then? Could you, would you, express it otherwise if the circumstances had proved to be quite different for you, I, or even those others? Is it the angle I describe which is problematical? Or was it your face at the window on that day, when the sunlight caught you, glancingly, and there were others who had similar thoughts, interrupting your own? You shifted aside, I recall, only to be replaced by other faces, which in their turn caught the eye of quite different passers-by. The consequence of which was that there came to be, in the end, a cast of thousands, if not many thousands – could it really have been that many or do I exaggerate or perhaps even hallucinate? – both at the window and then beneath, all staring up, and others, fleetingly, coyly, glancing back, both wanting to be seen and not wanting to be seen – as is the way with such as ourselves.

This is only the beginning of the little that I have to say. You tell me it is not little at all. You are wrong, many times wrong, and in several quite different respects. This is the start, the first step, in a very particular direction whose general aim, in the end, is to clarify everything with which I have been involved. It is a wiping of the windshield, an abluting of the body, the smashing of a god down from his pedestal. Yes, it is all those things and many more, and you must forgive me for the fact that from time to time it seems to come crowding, unstoppably urgent, as if all must be told far too quickly, as if there is some kind of a blind panic rising up in me. Seek out a measure of calmness in your response. That would be of help to both of us.

I queue for hours at a time on a day such as today. And at the end of the day, at the end of the queue, when all the crowds are dispersed, swept from a room like dust and cobwebs by no less a person than George Herbert (poet), who still croons contentedly amidst the snoozy piety of the seventeenth century, there is nothing left to bargain for. It has all gone. It has all been eaten, soundly masticated. All savaged away into nothingness. All sung in unison, and thence transported to the skies, where my eye climbs through narrow and ever changing spaces between the clouds, wondering whether I missed something, and what that something might have been, pledging that, next time, or the time after that, I would arrive in time to achieve my goal. Which is what exactly? Let the dumb-cluck of waterfowl be gone!

Did you make this – this moment, I mean – as much as you might ever have wished? There is so much cramming to be done, in these days of contumely. It is such a wonder that we stand here at all, so hard done to by the after-echo of so much silence. And then, just a minute, pardon me, you need not have said it at all. You could have declared it all over, and given yourself a bit of peace for a change. It was your choice, all along, you threw the dice, you made the call, you reached across to her, across all those yawning distances, didn't you? I have only your word for it, of course. It seemed, well, inevitable. There was no choice. I woke up to life bawling like a banshee in a cupboard, held upside down, mid-air, by the legs, twisting and writhing and wrenching around like some strung up gobbet of meat in the butcher's shop. That's how I was, utterly without dignity. And so it has remained. Only clothes ensure a modicum of dignity, and where are they, in the end, where are they?

We both breathed on it. We both wanted to look, so much, but the glass was fogged, and we merely stood there, hours long, hanging over, waiting for a change in the weather. I wish there had been more of us, but there were not. I wish that the circumstances had been slightly different, that there had not been such a world of unease drifting up as high as our shoulders and then back again like the idle washing of waves, but there was not. Where was the audience on that day? I have never been able to establish a credible reason for its absence. There was no justification for such a poor attendance when we had rehearsed so intensively, up to the moment of your arrival, and even beyond. You could say that we are still rehearsing, even today, long after the opportunity has been lost. And you – even you – had not arrived. You had boycotted, as one, the performance, and – let me tell you now for no one else will say it for me – had you not shown me – shown us – such disrespect, you would have witnessed the finest performance of your entire life. No, I do not brag. I state a fact.

There are no such things as hate-filled words. I do not deal in them. They are not of my nature. I have purged myself, repeatedly, which is why I can stand here in front of you, in all innocence, and declare: I am ready to go off now, to surrender everything that I have always been. Take me with you if you have the time, the space, the inclination – remember how you used to sweep your arm out to the side, somewhat balletically, so that I should precede you from the kitchen, with all the dishes heaped high on the tray in front of me, as if this were some ceremonial act, known only to the two of us, the breadth and the depth of its significance. Which is why I always said to you, as I glanced back to see you, always frozen there in that lovely posture: I am one amongst your number. Or not, as the case may be. I may be feigning again – except that I do not feign because I am always preying upon myself, looking out for the little and the large, keeping abreast of myself, seeking some reassurance as to my own authenticity, we might say, the two of us together, in a unison of sorts, if we were pushed. Which is not much. I have never dealt in much. It has always narrowed, little by little, day by day. I have watched it narrowing until all I have now is this, that which you see here in front of you, a man befogged, stranded, scrabbling, desperately scrabbling, on a roof, dirty-fingered, gripping the beauty of a bunch of terracotta tiles, French, of my particular allegiance, much rained on. I may lie here today again. It may not have been quite sufficient, ever, that which I supped from your hand. You never gave me enough. Was that it? Do not wrench me away, for all the danger I am in. I need this situation. It is a very satisfying summary. It is enough just to be here, to smell the scent of lavender, to bite into an August fig, how soft and penetrably sweet they always were, those August figs, even when wasp-riddled. I fell only once, and then, after that, and it was such a time in coming because time moves slow when you are staring at the ceiling, I never went up there again because you forbade it, you, in your kindness of heart, always a little stern and, unlike myself, never unruly. The gate opened on you that morning when I was lying on my side and looking straight across at the wall, being absorbed into the wall, in all its fulness of being. There is nothing quite like a wall for taking you, giving you that sense of complete absorption into itself.

You healed me. Or I healed myself, by merely waiting long enough for the train to pass by. We stood, side by side, with our bicycles, next to the lock, and listened to the curve of that whistle on the air, so high and so languorously long and slow in the air. I had a wish just then to be nowhere but there, and my wish had been granted, as if by some miracle of high summer. High summer's miracle, unchanging. And then it all slipped away, as if we were so many props to be struck, balsa wood, of the utmost flimsiness, gim-crack – which we were, of course. Props. Mere props. Off to the lumber room, into the eternal patience of the dark. It is all I ever asked of you, to be with me, hand in hand, in the patience of the dark. So much bunkum, you were so ready with words of that kind, words to sluice out my mouth, rid it of all its excess, all its ridiculousness. I am the equal of my age, you said, which has never been much. As if you knew. As if you of all people ever knew. When you spoke, I spoke with you. My words were an echo of yours. They were bedfellows. I made a sculpture, that morning – how did I do it, I of all people? – of icicles snapped from the eaves, which were barely within reach of my hands. They fell and, before it all melted, I set my hands to work as if I barely owned them, such was the speed, such the dexterity, of my fingers. And now so much is beyond my reach. All powers of description have left me, as if I have no use for them any more. Someone asked it of me just the other day, as I was bending to tie a silly shoe – how one does laugh at a shoe! – and I murmured that it was no longer to be. It was that simple. Nothing requires much effort. It is as if all things fall forwards now, sighing-slow, into their particular places in the public square, wind-swept, with its benches, and then they doggedly remain where they have fallen, and some, idling along as one does on a Sunday with an empty pocket or two to account for, come to watch or to comment or to poke about – or merely to murmur or to mumble. Why not choose? Why not desist from choosing? I call it gum-chewing. They are all at it. I call it postponement. There is nothing quite so widespread as a general postponement, it has been said, repeatedly, by some. Others are waiting to set ridicule in motion – any old box of tricks will do.

You paper the room with your racket. You take up the bucket and the paste and the water and you mix it. And then you slather it all over, walls, floor, ceiling, everywhere, and it is always there, the unceasing racket of you, squealings, grindings, gruntings, blaahings unceasing. There is no sponge large enough to stuff up your mouth. And what you say is what you have always said and what you are always saying and what you will always say, the relentless crowing of your self-affirmations, always the same words, slightly rearranged, but the self-same words oncoming, like the ceaseless raging of the waters. And I fall and get tossed about, and I flail with my arms and I spew you out, repeatedly, day after day, spit you out, vomit you forth, the sickening bile of you, and I never quite rid myself of you because there is always so much of the same of you, and always oncoming. The flat, hard, merciless hammering down of your words. The noise of the ugly boom and belch of your voice, which will never cease to be heard. The disgusting racket of your voice, unstoppable, unstillable, terrible, wheedling, unforgettable.

On that day, it had all stopped, all the pain of it had gone away. I was lying side-on, in the air, counting my breaths, not urging them along, merely letting my lungs settle, and then slowly expand again, in an almost involuntary fashion. And it was all so easy. There were no solutions, rapid or difficult, required of me, no posing of awkward questions. I was no longer standing in a room amongst so many, looking for a place to cling to. I myself was being clung to, buoyed aloft on heaven's breath. What is this? I asked of myself in a whisper – because I feared to disturb the peace of it all. What is this? There were no further questions to be asked. The years of questioning had all ended. I would like to pause for a moment and describe all this to you, with the utmost care and attention, in order to permit you to enter in, almost to become that which I have been. I would like to tell you: this is how it all was, how I knew it then. I would like to do that above all things else. Readiness is of the moment.

Yes, perhaps. You were the one to question me. I had assumed that there would be a certain inevitability about it all. Are we alone in that? Or, to put it slightly differently: is each of us quite singular in that respect? Or are there several in that predicament? The corridors were full of children, I noticed that immediately, a surge of rather poor children with sore mouths, strange swellings, rags for bodily adornment. There was a certain shame about it all, I could see that, almost immediately, because they were sealing their mouths with their hands. I did not know what to say to any of them – it would be perfectly useless, I recognised, to shout out loud: what good am I here, now? – and it was for this reason that I hung back in the shadows, and began to compose something rather different, a piece for a chorus of two or three, gentle voices gently interweaving, like threads of silk. I could see the chapel in which it would be sung. I saw a man step forth with the music. And then I saw a fleeting look of perplexity on his face – it gripped hold of him for seconds only – just before – and then he resumed to stride forth boldly. Why such perplexity then? The fact is that I shared it. (It would also be true to say that I had added my own note of anguish and dismay.) You see, my friend: there were no choristers, no listeners, and no chapel.

Is there any reason to begin again when all is resolved to our mutual satisfaction, the drawers all empty, the floors clean swept, the yard cleared of all its rubbish? My mouth is empty of words for a change. I am standing out in the air. Two or three are approaching, all refreshingly unfamiliar. They are waving bottles at me. I run for the bucket. I plonk it down in the forecourt. I crawl inside it. I rock it from side to side like a drunken sailor whose ocean has dried to a lick of salt. Is there not at least once? And could there not be this once once again if we were all to shake hands in amity and pull together?

This much at least is known, that you arrived. And I was not there because I was not. Why more than that? Why not keep it simple? Why stretch the string until it aches and then smothers us? There is not so much to be said for the human condition, never has been. It has always been sighs, shrugs of the shoulder, fag ends, always that little – or that much. I do not marshall pigs, dogs, cows. That has never been within my earthly remit.

Must all luminaries of any particular stamp park their cars in our bedroom, where the clothes live their happy lives and the cockroaches croon for the rhapsody of our biddable autumnal sunsets? There is filth beyond measure, beyond the reach of composure. I scrabble around in the dictionary, always displeased, always returning to the same two or three. Satisfaction is a particular favourite. Satisfaction once crowned me, and I remonstrated by way of a brief kiss to the cheek. More sting, peremptory, than kiss.

It is all for the asking. The point is never to refuse because if you refuse, they push you aside, and you are obliged to begin again, which is always so vexatious when you had been on the point of beginning. So do not lack for courage. Steel yourself and go armed with, say, a bunch of anemones on the doorstep, and hold them out with good cheer, eagerly, with an exaggerated smile on your face as if you might wish to please, because a lady always loves an anemone, and if by any chance she does not... The appetite sickens and then dies. I need to tell you this because you are here with me, and our time together is strictly limited.

I respond, always, to the ghost wind. I let it lift me. A lifting is needful from time to time, when one lacks the capacity to choose, as I do. That is why I am here because now I am fit for nothing but this, an accounting of sorts, in this garden, as I sit on this wall, idly nodding to the drifting populace, picking apart the meaning of words, a veritable Humpty Dumpty to your Alice. Or you could choose to ignore me and just let me get on with it. There is much sifting to be done, I recognise that. There are boxes unopened for years which I am enjoying the anticipation of opening at last. I both know what is in there and do not. It is a bit of a guessing game because what you say that you see is not necessarily in agreement with my interpretation – or even my knowledge of this rough and tumble world I have lived through. How ignorant am I? And how ignorant are you? May I ask? What did you wilfully choose to ignore when the troops were setting out their stall in the market place? Were you merely a form of light entertainment – or did you see yourself as a challenge of sorts? Did you merely live and let live? And did I? Or did I brandish a dangerous fist? Set down a marker to be remembered by someone or other, someone other than my own heroic or perhaps pusillanimous self, I mean? These are important matters. Much deep digging is required. You must not succumb to boredom or, worse, sleep, just because the hour is late and the moment of final confrontation, wheat-from-chaffing, ever pressing. Have another double espresso – and on me this time because it is I who

have obliged you to suffer in this way. You may
have noticed that I have not yet offered you an
apology because I would not know how. It is not
within my nature. I am a bludgeon, a bulldozer, a
timely, slow-spinning brick through your window,
make no mistake of it, boyyo.

It is a catastrophe. It is all a catastrophe. That is
why there is so much water on this floor, and it is
ever spreading. It is the water of a nation's tears,
and no mops or brooms could ever be sufficient to
deal with it. There is just too much of it. And I too
am helpless. Incapable of offering you the kind of
explanation you might expect of me because, after
all, it has happened on my watch, while I was
engaging you in conversation at the back door,
idling the hours away like the careless fool that I
am. So to that extent I am at least partially
responsible because I might have been more
vigilant. I might have looked out of the window,
even a quick, furtive glance might have done, and
then back into the shadows, and even anticipated
what was about to happen, and I did not, I lay on
my back, I slept, I drummed my fingers, I muttered
words. I shuffled a pack of cards at four o'clock in
the afternoon and played patience with myself
until all that street noise faded away into

inaudibility. That is what sort of a man I am, should you now choose to judge me.

I have told you this until I can barely bring myself to say it again. The exchequer deals with the money. I have left it all in his safe keeping. I have no use for it. Food rises to the mouth as if in a dream of satisfied appetite, and drink to the lips. And, hey presto, that's it. There is no other story to tell. And he? He? Yes, he is a he. The exchequer is the very model of benignity. He deals with it as he sees fit. Most of all, he leaves me alone to... to tend the garden, to sort the mellifluous camellias from the equally mellifluous lobellias. And, no, they do not grow on either side of the sycamore because there isn't one. There has never been a sycamore here. I have never stooped, not even once, to such levels of vulgarity. Nor, needless to say, have you, ha!

It has always been a loose conjoining. There have been many rooms spoken for, days, weeks before. They bar you. They stand with their arms folded, the stern-faced, muscular men, and block the way.

There is nothing for it but to turn back and live it all again. One does baulk at first. One does crave the promise of the future. But if all that is to be denied, what more is there to be said or done? Why not gently sink into the waves? I took her to a small seaside town, out of season, to watch how the people flow along the promenade, out of season. It was a melancholy display of such as ourselves on those days of utmost futility, more stuttery, more hesitant, more shuddery, and infinitely slower. There was almost no staring out to sea. The sea was a painted backdrop, a nothing that was real at all at all. I have done with the sea for now. How could it be so? I asked myself as we closed the door of the carriage.

Just before we left, I had stepped onto the pier in my short trousers and run pell-mell towards the mysterious turbaned wizard enclosed in his tall glass box. I slipped in a coin and watched his hands circling over the possibilities, circling so slowly, more slowly even than the circling of the moons of Saturn. Eventually he picked up a sliver of paper in his claw hand and dropped it down the chute. My heart was pounding, as it always used to pound. I picked it up. I read it. I committed it to memory, and then I returned to you, full of this inner mystery. Or should I say: I returned to look for you. You too, I guess, were looking, somewhere, though not necessarily for me.

Now that it has all gone away at last, and the customary silence has descended, give me a little brightness again. It is not enough to stand in the dull corner all evening, as if I am an object to be condemned for being nothing but myself. There has to be a lightening, some sounds of good cheer, perhaps even cheering. Wait a minute though, was I not asking for silence just now? Or did I mistake my meaning?

The Indifferent Garden

I mistook you then for a garden, an unkempt garden needless to say, flung about, impatient to fructify. I dragged my feet as I walked through you. I dipped into the shade beneath your trees, the fig tree, the cherry tree, and the catalpa, which overlooks, you may remember so acutely, as do I, our doorway, accentuating its notes of such bright green astonishment when the sun shines through. I looked out to see you watching me there. I was in the midst of you, trying to make sense of you once and for all, rapping on your bark, examining the translucency of your leaves, enquiring, and even pleading, to be let in to your innermost chamber. And still you resisted me. Still you held back and said not one word. Even the wind's sigh, when it came, was not your sigh but some other's. And so I returned to the house, and I waited in my chair at the table for the seasons to assume an attitude calmer and more kindly. And, by and by...

Those days were several, needless to say, and I caught up each one of them with much impatience, not wanting to say too much, not wanting to make what might amount, in the end – in the wrong hands – to a final admission. Did you show much forbearance? Could you conjure such a quality? I leant back, generally speaking, against much generous daylight, thankful at last tc be welcoming some breathing sense of finality. What would be made of it all in the end? I asked myself as, leaving for good, I plunged down and down into the valley. The light, by then, had grown sullen and moribund.

There were always spaces, generous spaces, between one note and the next. It especially pleased me, to be able to inhabit them with such an attitude of welcoming, to move into them, side-on, as a small child might slip through the smallest space imaginable. I had become, yet again, yes, that small child, with such a boundless appetite for headlong adventure. Had you known me like that at all, when you looked at me, seated in a chair, or pacing the room from end to end, so impatient to bring about our final resolution? Did you look when you looked? Or did you look beyond your own looking?

There is likely to be no end to it at all. I for one

have no reason to be leaving just yet, having just arrived, and so fresh these days, with the full scent of usefulness in my hair, on my clothes. No one speaks of a new man, least of all myself, given this predicament – an entire garden, for example, for which to hold oneself responsible, with rain squalls coming on, and several roof tiles unstable over this old, oh dear, house of sorts. My beginning, needless to say, has never been my end.

What manner of a man is this, he who comes walking towards me, and then veers off just as I open my mouth to speak? What would he have said back to me, had I had the rare opportunity to speak to him, how would he have countered it, my ambition, my intense forward strikes, swingeing around at first rather helplessly, to the eye and the teeth? He would have registered a degree of flaccidity, I reckon, and even impotence, because there is no other way to go when you are wholly determined to lash out and win the prize.

Take it. Refuse it. Parry it. Or stuff it away. There is always that pocket beyond and behind one's innermost pocket. Many times I have guessed at it.

Many times I have come close – as a wind can close-shave at the cheek, and almost remove flesh from bone. Quite terrifying when it happens. I have been quite at a loss to know what to do in such a situation. Sit down. Take your time. There is oodles of it, don't you know? They have hung you out to dry, as they do with the old. There is no use for you any longer. And there is no advice to be had either because the train has just pulled out, and you have been left with your small handkerchief again. Limp now, for staunching the bitterest of tears. I pity you. I feel for you too when I do not despise you. By way of a welcome distraction, tear off a sheet of newsprint and let us all know what is happening today. Prove yourself good for something.

*

I picked up a matchstick in the foyer – between acts two and three, I believe. I picked it up and twiddled it between my fingers. One or two noticed, and quite quickly, quite noiselessly, they passed on by because they could see that a large embarrassment was brewing. It would not have been difficult. And they had not even seen the glass at my back! That prop was to come in useful a little later, by which time it was empty. Of course it was, dullard! An old pro such as myself doesn't miss that kind of a trick. Sweating though! Sweating! That was only the half of it. You see, having got this far, I had to make it clear exactly how I would sum up the rather unnerving situation, were I to be asked, and I knew that I *would* be asked because I was the last in line – the bell had rung long ago, the corridor was completely empty by now – and perhaps I was also, let's be truthful, let's get to the bottom of things, perhaps I was also the most futile looking, the most lacklustre, the most slipshod, the most ungainly. How does one put it to oneself? I don't know. Sometimes one passes beyond all knowing when in the grip of this strange mood of serenity, years later. It must be years by now. Nothing is quite tangible any more, which is a kind of relief, to be letting go. Would you not think so if you had had the patience to stay and listen to me? Even just the once? You always had to *do your own thing*, didn't you? What an ugly, ugly phrase that is – and so insulting!

There is always this question of usefulness dinning at the inner ear. Are you useful? Is this useful? To what good use can we put it? It never ends. I don't know what to say any more. There are such rags and tatters, and all so carelessly strewn about, such fag ends everywhere these days, scraps of memory, careless, illegible jottings, bits of unfinished business, yawning pot holes in the road, half built structures cluttering up the sky, and all going nowhere. Everything, it seems to me, is almost entirely useless, or is falling into uselessness even as we look at it or stare it down. I am so adept at these rather fierce starings down.

The other day I had drawn it out for a little longer than usual, the late evening hour in the garden. I had stopped the sun going down. I had stopped that sudden, oncoming chill by steadying my glass on the table. A simple trick. The easiest in the book. By sheer force of will? Perhaps. Perhaps I have these powers of prestidigitation. You thought it a joke, of course. You went indoors anyway. You saw what I didn't see, you said. You knew that night had come on – or would, within a matter of minutes, you said, quite brusquely, as if what I was saying might be construed as a personal insult. So I sat out there, all night, enjoying all those tiny remnants of daylight suspended between the stars. Twenty-two of them there were, and all of differing sizes.

And that pretty well amounts to it. The gulf is always too great between here and there. To infinity. Accidents have a way of imposing themselves on unexpected days, when the sun has been peeking up – or, at worst, trying to, which is good enough by my lights. I always say – would you like to hear it again, albeit tedious in the extreme? – that I would have offered it to you for a second time had you asked. There was nothing to stand between us – except for the fence which is, of course, a given in these situations of hypothetical rivalry. I simply do not know where life went. Did you make off with it? I can scarcely believe it of you. Unless, of course, you are not you, which is quite a different category, one that begins just beyond the mist over there. You know it, goofy. Don't you pretend. I would have lifted it all out cleanly and just left it, facing the sea. No, *outfacing* the sea because the sea always needs a challenge. Had you arrived just then, as promised, you would have known all about it. I would not have needed to tell you. There are imps in the side pocket, small ones, crushable between thumb and finger. Go to it, my sometime friend. Nearness is always a dream of nearness because the truth of it is that you almost never rise from your bed. You expect everything to be done for you, even the thinking. Who owns thinking? Do you? Should we all take responsibility for the way the world cranks along? Dear old world of has-beens and might-have-beens and should-have-beens. And then there is you, just off to the side, like a bent nail, and always so ugly in spite of all the make-up. I just don't know what to do about it any more. It all has to end or, as they put it these days: let them re-boot it! I would stand in anyone's way. My opinions count for not a jot. Nor for a chewable length of hemp. Go your way, pretty tricycle – if anyone can afford you. You are so completely useless. I wish I could say the same of myself. At least it would be something definite, something eagerly graspable – like an ice cream which must always stay frozen in the cone (geometry), no matter how many times you may choose to subject it to all those furious lickings. Who stripped away the hours when we were doing nothing more unpardonable than merely stand here? It seems totally unacceptable to be flayed in public like a beast going gingerly on all fours or a god way up there on a pedestal, never breathing a word.

It is just the way the rhythm of boxes happens to tumble out on these kinds of mornings, always steadily, never one in front of another. No unseemly jostling as between thee and me, we oldsters wielding as many rusting crankshafts as we can buy for a muck–rake full of stinking gold, and all fresh off the shelf! How I exceeded myself just then. Let me expel a little wind now – if you will excuse me. Just for the sake of it, you must understand. There is nothing of which man is not capable. And you have seen it all, more than once, on many sad occasions, with flowers and molten tears and deep, deep holes in the ground. Who would stare without being approached first? It would be unseemly. At best, there would need to be hesitation of the most solemn kind. Your broom yesterday swept away all frivolity. That was my gift to you, you do understand. That, and all the crockery for which I no longer had any use, because there were no aunts or cousins or thieves or anything similar any longer. I had grown un-fond of all of them. So, to repeat myself again – how tedious this is! – you got all the crockery, and there was no real need to throw it at you. That was born of the unspoken need to give exercise to an arm which had been growing redundant since the end of the Cold War. That long ago. Were you alive just then, even twitchingly, beside the road perhaps, amongst tiny shreddings and out-featherings of roadkill?

Make it two. Why such meagreness when so many shots ring out from so many different directions? I am a man who reaches out for abundance every livelong day. Just call me sir or waste not your words. The choice is simple. As is my life these days. It has not always been so. Once I was all twisted up and round and back. And then I ironed myself out. Some god – in which I did not believe, of course – spoke through me. On the out-breath only. Why be wasteful when time is so pressing, and there are so many questions still to be answered from the outfield? Steady is life, and so spasmodic. Sometimes it seems to stretch away beyond the pallid kiss of tedium. Then it does not. It is all bunched up here at the knee. You find that you cannot even leave the table. The very air consists of dollops of, sloppings of, glue, and all crooning at you, as if you were alive and idling quixotically – in, say, the 1950s again – without hope of amend. You are even glued to the chair again, having freed yourself only the other day! How did it all come swinging round again, the old predicament, the old entrapment? And yet you do recognise, when it happens, that you are not yourself, that this is not your story. The mirror is telling a different tale. And who would not wish for that? Money is not the half of it.

Deliver me from here. Let it all be peeled away. Why not? Why not enquire after the best at the office door, join the long queue down the street? At least there will be a chance of meeting fellow sufferers, and even of exchanging life opportunities, or three of them at the very least.

Steep-sided ravines and, of course, valleys into which to plunge. A simulacrum of nature at its most compliant, prepared to be written of. You asked it of me again and again, to be outwreathing it all, you commented. And yet nothing happened of any consequence. I have your word for it. You were with me just then, standing there. We breathed each other's breath. I have the nail to prove it. I also asked you back from somewhere else, from which nook you did not return, a tidy, warm, old ingle-nook of a place needless to say, within all our remembrance, and in Dudley too to cap it all. Let me say it again so that you are forced into listening the second time around. I called you back from somewhere else. It all amounts, in the end, to losing. That is what I told you. Your history is still here beside me for all that you have tried and tried to rid yourself of me. Friendliness must count for nothing in the end. The gate closes. The gate opens. To walk this road is not to ask for forgiveness. To be here, at least, is not to pay homage to sanctity. Or you may not choose the consequences. That is entirely your prerogative. There are ins and there are outs. I, meanwhile, caught you back from there. I also taught you nothing. A steady resting place. Nothing less than that. Curious enough to be spoken of quickly and wilfully. Three clear moments of acceptance took hold of me just then, and each one quite as overbearing as the last. Ouch. And its after-echo. So wilful.

Why did you call me then if you had no wish to speak to me? Why did you call me if you had no wish to be present in front of me? What are these days for then? Are they useless without conversation of any kind, or do they come into their own when the street clears, and even the last of those songbirds I love so much to be hearing has returned to Madagascar? I wish I had no further questions for you. I wish I had no need in the end, once again, to invoke your name, because it is always so perfectly useless to me. It always proves, in the end, to be such a disappointment. *This is the outer limit*, those were your last words.

I puzzled over them so. I even praised you for them. I called them wise or perhaps not so foolish. I gave you the benefit of the doubt.

To smite at the ground just so. To make this gesture of oncoming. And then to walk away again just as quickly as you had come. There are spasms to be gone through. That is what I would ask of you, no less than that. And a course of fever, to which I am inclined daily. Whose day, if not yours and ours? Bonded once again. Together! We need to make it so. We need to embrace it as if it had always been here, even when the last of these seconds has failed us. You are so puny. Your resting place will be equally easy. There is such an assortment of inconsequential nooks and crannies. There is also a course in the higher mathematics available to the least of us just beyond the door of the scullery.

Your ring was never my ring. Mine was a neck ring, tight as could be, almost strangulatory. Yours spun on your finger end like a firework. Such crowds gathered to see! Such offerings flung down to the female deity! I felt so proud of you then that I drank down my coffee far too quickly and suffered the consequences for many hours after. Are we not thigh-deep in it, both of us, or is all this an illusion? I have guessed. Your turn now. Ranks come and go. Just a few. Far too many. Where do we fit in? We are the observing men. We do our best. We are essential to its success. They check our arithmetic by wetting their finger ends and then just going at it. Why not? Wouldn't you if you were asked? But the sad truth is that no one is asking. You are on your own out here, with a flickering night light. And this is why I choose to pity you. The cost is immaterial. Fencing the air is better. It clarifies – like the best of our dreams. Yours is not. Nor mine. Do pardon the level of presumption. The church window yawns ajar, expectant of the callow thief. In it or not. There is no denying that I asked you because just then I was not sleeping. I had jerked myself awake moments before, and I was pulling on my sentences as if they were my grandfather's long johns. It was all proving so cumbersome because of my love of long words. Had you made such a statement before? And did it become you? I am seduced by those avenues running down to the Seine. That is where you must take me in my favourite bath chair, when I prove to be too old in the end. Irrespective of wars, conquests, atrocities, it is still there I must go, should you have the inclination, which I very much doubt. Click, clickety click goes the bait in the jar. We do not hear. Others do. Many go fishing every day. It is a national hobby. To be stabbed in the back with a rod, that is a favoured form of death amongst the fishing fraternity. I would go for it too, were I not out of favour, were I not my least favourite tune in the juke box. One or two still come running when they hear it. I do. I am the first amongst men. My eyes moonshine with pleasure to be so spoken of. Who would not? What dregs, what drudges would not wish to be hauled forth and praised in this way? It is the end of things now, you know, or as near as dammit. Was that not declared yesterday, when I was feeding the ducks? Is that why so many were absent, and so much sunlight had drawn away in displeasure? You are not mine, you know. We are not twinned infamies. That was the billboard speaking, bellowing even, without any prompting, as they do from time to time. Tea with a bun please. Tea mellow and lip-luscious. Drawn back from the teeth like that Pharaoh lost amidst the waves, so tragic and so just, such a reasonable outcome for so much random wetness, urgh. I never asked for you again. In fact, I never asked for you the first time. You chanced along entirely of your own accord. That, after all, is what you do – it is *all* that you do – or rather *did* because you do it no longer, having been resigned to a double bed since the bench mark declared it so. Such a bland air of finality. Few would have guessed it, we must surely agree.

I turned all this coffined confinement into such a snappy tune, and all so broadly taken up. I could have died just to see it. Were you there beside me on that bench, addressing the royal waterfowl, or am I just guessing? When you speak to no one, no reply is quite good enough. There is always such an anchoring, such embedding. Merely to be here, without restraint or hindrance. The noising abroad of it all proves impossible of course because the message fritters away on the air, at the least expulsion of breath. You were not alone when I named you. That was myself I was referring to. Such solace. Such hole-in-corner business. A testamentary bequest, that is how we referred to it. Not mine but yours, and all for the asking – or the giving, to be perfectly simple. Who would be confused when all the clouds withdraw as if at a single mighty clap of the hands?

Umbrageous Interludes

Was it dread? Is that what you called it? Why conjure such a word when your teeth were gleaming so magically? This floor is to be countered. The rest can be discarded, given to the readily impatient. I have no time for all of that. My wrists are bare and bleeding. Let the smooth notes run on as we surf along with them. That is captivity of a kind - and yours too, I suspect, if you would only open up to me. Even a clavicle would do, fine and dandy. Does it squeal when you prise it apart? Are you that brazen these days? I wish I knew. I know so little. Speaking of myself, that is. Changing the subject rather hastily: to see right through, that must be any eager man's ambition, stiff meadow walkers that we are always destined to be.

Right. I asked you, and you failed to reply. You refused me. On the contrary, you are not to be put down. This, once again, is the test of wakefulness, vigilance, no matter how home-spun it always proves to be these days. Were you responsible for these particular waves? I embraced them. They knew my name. The rest is a form of prattle, with which I am always quite comfortable. Who would not opt for the home base, when discomfort is flung around so carelessly? It is what you do to yourself – and *with* yourself, of course. That is all that we amount to, given that I talk in my own voice, which seldom reaches across more than a single valley. Are you still familiar with the Ribble? Me too. Stretched out so bare. And so magisterial. I grasp at a word or two, and then I hook them on, each one, just so. I am also a tad hobbled these days, that is the truth of it. I have seen far, and now I see so little.

As for yourself, who could ever presume to speak? You were tall. You were short. You were here. You were gone. You held the dimensions of a single and quite substantial house, balanced in the palm of your hand. Such miracle-making! Of which I am incapable. Call me servile if you so wish. I run when I come. I never walk or slouch. Mark all that down, quite ruthlessly, you strap-hanging kiddo, as evidence of eagerness, to which I would give the lie if you dug a little deeper. Which you may wish to do. It is of course your prerogative. Nightly. Daily. It must all run on, fiddly faddly and away, beyond the distant horizon. There is nothing else for it. I stand directly across from it, wheeling my arms. Staunch. Ever abiding. Lips pursed. Jungle escapee, and so easily. Like slipping out of a side pocket. The cunning of it all, the sheer dexterity too, are boundless. Come here a little sooner then. I will always be waiting. There will always be a superfluity of umbrageous moments for you to batten onto. Wear a poncho for style. Me too! If yet another exquisite opportunity does not slide away into the ditch. Who would wallow when the neck could be stretched taut?

Oh no, not again. You did say so. Why should I deny you? Is there any space here for denial, with all these clouds running over like so many rude, scampering children? I for one have had enough of it all. Just so. Rightly so. Your call. The opening gambit only. A fib in a nest. You quietly disgust me, you know, with your makeshift habits, pushing the planks around the floor as if everything were so easy all the time, and you had all the time in the world to make it happen, braggart that you are. I cannot make it any more. Popular tunes push up against me like unruly children. Stop them then! Would I had the strength so to do, old fellow of mine, drunk in the quad again without bicycles, curtains or ladder. What do we all amount to in the end? Do you? No one dares pose such a question because posing was so *de rigueur* in the old days, which are long gone, of course. I wish I could see as far as the tent pole. It recedes whenever I approach it like a grieved lover. Too many opportunities for so little noise, I hear you say without fear of interruption. Favours are flying again, unhindered as flags along the street. Don't we all love them? No we do not, porker! Someone said once that that dream of you was never a dream of you at all. It was a dream of me, with iced topping. Come in from the rain again. Seize a little shelter as if it were your birthright. You will inherit by and by, when fate or futurity swing in your direction. You just have to show some patience as you work your toes about, never expecting too much of yourself. Codgers get tipped into the ground. It's as simple as that. We walk on by twirling our parasols and crooning lightly. On any such day as today. A genuine gift from the packaging warehouse, which has meant good news for so many. More rats on the ice rink. More general jollity. Why believe if your card is declined repeatedly? I would ask myself that too. It is all a matter of such urgency. There is no space for you here. You have lost, and you must pack yourself away and be gone. It was all too soon for you, ho hum. Too soon, as all the bland hills echo-ed. And, don't forget this telling detail, a multitude of hills to climb by morning, in the drizzle, without companions to speak of. Or, correction, be spoken of. There are many companions not to be spoken of, and I have forgotten all their names. The sweep was comprehensive. Call it nihilism. I would go along with that. You can add my dice to the bundle. See if I care. It is none of my business what you do with your cat when my back is turned, ninny.

Forsaken or abandoned. Pushed to the side. And I am still at it. What could ever stop me? I am into it now, arms pumping for the line, which is fast approaching. Wish me the luck of every passing moment! Spare me one of your glances if you do not find yourself over-committed. Wearisome, burdensome are the demands of the ear, my friend. Take cover – or nothing will happen at all. The sack will merely empty itself out. I would opt for the latter because it is a little easier when you are in your condition, always a mite threadbare about the elbows, as we always used to say of you when your ears were beyond reach of the truth, which was often. Then there is the question of penitence – should you wish to go into all of that too. There is a box to climb into with no evident exit route. That might be just the stuff for you, *jongleur* that you are in this hilly village of stiff-necks, on a grey day such as this one. The stranger's song, it has to be said, has been sung once too often. There are too many buses away from it. Choose: 9, 16, 143, 74. None of them idle, all are filthy needless to say. What do you expect? It is you who have chosen to live here.

Sometimes I rise up wishing, nothing but that. And then I stop and quickly think of the consequences. A searing blankness. Deliveries far too many and far too bold and far too loudly outspoken. May a plague of tinnitus descend upon you! Snuff it all out then. Pay no heed to candle wax on the finger ends. Let us all think again. What about making it all up? Forever? Why not? Hold your ground. Give them for what! Would that be an option? Your childishness, for example, and how you dribbled once down her cuff when your arms were flapping around uselessly. I could have made something of you then, had I been able to reach you. We could have lingered for an hour or two at least in that warm vestibule, preparing for the good times to come seething along again. Did I die before you were born? Could that be the problem, the very reason why I am not able to bring you into sharp focus, you mist-wallower you? I would have died to make it happen, but, excuse me for a moment, I was dead already, in all death's enveloping peacefulness, in all its oh-so-soothing thank-you-for-everythingness! And then, almost immediately after they had swung the five-barred gate open and let the horses back into the field with plentiful supplies of hay, you came tripping along, wholly incapable of being aware of me, and consequently singularly happy in all your childish pridefulness. That is your story then, if I may be so bold as to tell it. Denial? Finger this carapace, lady.

The station lay back, just across the road from here, and so open to the air, lingering there in all its gentle passivity. A few of us lay across the track and waited. There were a few mushrooms by way of companions, fine, up-thrusting beasts, fashioned of iron and human grit, which the elders construed as water towers. When the train paused to observe us, we merely waved and wished it well. Back on board, tea was being served. The ceiling depended in its own odd way, all honey and false favours, all entirely admirable to its unquestioning admirers, and the loose change just went on passing and passing from hand to hand until we fell blind – wholly stricken, as if some god had done it to us – with staring at too many winking coins, and all scattered abroad in our favour, poor losers that we were. Such poor losers. I feel ashamed of myself again today. I simply could not have done it.

The furniture never stood up for itself. It played the victim card, always. Victims of this kind provoke no sorrow, and so we burnt it, to the very last stick, and, in later life, sat hunched over on rocks scattered around near the door. It was not pleasant. It was also salutary, a stiff lesson in self-improvement, we all agreed.

Steep slopes make for little comfort when night draws in and eyes clang shut. You crawl on all fours when that happens. You wail a little. You call for the biggest beast of all favours, which lifts you onto its back and bears you along to the jetty, from where, oh luck, you take the light-scudding skiff to the mainland. And there you are deposited. No, it is not here after all. This is a place that drifts sideways in common with the tide, you have already noticed. Chagrin. It is somewhere else then. There is a mere reaching forth with clumsy hands, and fumbling, much quiet fumbling and scratching at brown paint. The dog scratch. The cat scratch. The rat scratch. Words do not fall in line. Something is not quite as it seems. All odd again, and all too familiar. Your name is on it, like a signature half rubbed out. Your name is on what though, when it is spoken out loud, nothing more than that? When you push at the air, as you do, it does not push back. Instead, you fall forward. And you are still falling forward. Is this a game or a calamity? You choose.

Stop to be spoken. Light tricks of the soon-to-be-breathed-out-loud, when windows impinge and scratch persistently at the edges, as if wholly uncaring. Fumble back into the pocket. Squeeze the pocket dry, my child. Let us know what happened, everything, before you began to question the way of it. I have no patience these days. Too much has been going on to prevent it ever happening without you. There is always too much of your special pleading. Come clean. Sluice yourself down of all indifference.

This was the meeting moment, surely, side on to the table. At a glance. At a guess. And so many voices! Wait till you've gone. That would be for the best. Then I can go too. Is this some dream of a wastrel? Me? Pull the other one, old pal of mine. You must be joking. We had it all before. You do not quite recall, do you? That makes it two to me and one to you. Easy arithmetic. Something fell away. Plonk. Barely if ever mentioned by the two or three who had been said to know you, in the bad old days. Or perhaps you do. Some days there is much more of it than usual, your raging banter, and how you always turned up trumps in the conservatory, one leg folded over another. My dream of you perhaps. Your dream of yourself, ever fading, ever drizzling away into the aether. When were you as you were always thought to be? By ourselves, that is. No one else was fooled. All your colleagues lined up to look askance. Immense. O'erlooking. Crabby too when you were not quite thinking clearly. What a tidal wave of opportunities always fell across you! You were always wanted now and then, more so now than then. I never quite said I loved you, though perhaps I meant to from time to time. Cracked cup, soonest mended. The old times were rough and soon over, we hurried towards them as the dockers ran towards the boats. Get those sacks off before it all perishes! Teetering down the gangplank, all bent of back, such dear old men in their tattered loin cloths. Barely covering the best and the worst. So fetchingly biblical. And now this, which is not at all as we had expected. The old days again, pushed creaking open. I do nod my head like a sage from time to time and wonder, and peck, peck and wonder. Too many gone. Too many hurrying on along the gantry. Splash. The end. Finality's grand resolution. Tautology. Hippopotami? Just as you wish. You are the conjuror, and I the mere audience, barely an audience at all, scattered about like peanuts frittered across the rug. I wish it not. Nor, wait a moment for me to explain, do I wish it for you because you only deserve what they throw at you, and it comes so steadily, with such a peaceful demeanour too as if music itself, in all its world-encompassing grandiosity, were this gift proffered to all of us. Don't look at me like that. Do not lean so. Your face will fall off into the tea cup. They will oblige you to leave before me, and now you have disappointed me by not yet arriving again, and I am pining and staring down at this watch, which forever requires adjustment. Did we fabricate it all for the best – or was most of it a guess, a summer's kiss, an autumnal keening over deep down mud? That is how you described it, always. I am shaken about. I am mixed in with the food and no one seems to notice – my absence or that slightly different taste. Such tomfoolery today when the telegraph wires are singing overhead so joyously. Who mentioned the birds again? They were never part of the partnership. We have no time for holding back. I do not know – I shall never know now – what it was about your gestures, how you could wipe me out with a single flourish. And then it all happened as we read in this book I am writing so assiduously - if we still have the sight to see by, which I very much doubt given your halting nature, how you shuffle towards me and then open up your palm again with gifts in abundance. You were always far too demonstrative, did I ever tell you that, amongst all the rest of the prattle? I said too much, but never the right things. Never matters *apropos* as they say, italicising the word for the sake of an extremity, dire indeed, you must surely agree, of finickiness. Your desk, with all its thoughts heaped up, just kept on moving around like one of those dodgem cars at the beach. You never stood still. You never sat still. You never caught up with them. And when you did, the words were always just beyond the reach of minute interrogation, as so many of them tend to be at these hectic moments of extreme forgetfulness. Did I die before you? And am I dead now? I doubt it! You should too. The questions just keep coming, the same ones I fear, whereas the grave, as we were slow-taught in seminary classes, is silent. Did you say it? Would you? Why hold back when you have always had so much to offer, so broad in the intellect's much more than fierce beam? Labouring man continues to heave a mattock in the field. Was that Millais? And did I embrace his beard that evening I met him? Would it have been going too far in a certain direction? As for you, you failed to honour your obligations at all. You missed ferry, coach, taxi, bus, and then you sicked up the banquet after I had paid for it all, on the nail, on the dot of nine, when they had always been so so demanding, those French paymasters with their serpent tongues. I am sorting out the boxes this morning to the charming ringing of bells, and it is all going well, I am pleased to report to you in this letter. Did you ever finish the last one? And would you describe your reply to my umpteen questions about your behaviour, now and then, as adequate? I would not. I demand supplementaries! Fist fights in the lobby again. All hurrying away from the truth, which is always so galling. This is not the moment to goad public opinion into rising up in open defiance, but why should tomorrow offer an even better opportunity? What is it about tomorrow? Have you even seen that far? Pusillanimity at the top. We are only as good as the single eye which opens. Last but not least there are the socks, and how you pull them on. Who would pay good money to see you, then or whenever? Even as a child you were a scoundrel, close-sifting all that sand from hand to hand, never owning up to so much back-storage in the meadow. Your dream, as usual, was paramount. You marched in front. Yes, you always insisted, as if your opinions counted. And so I chose to live a different life altogether. I even changed my name, and twisted my mouth to one side in a certain way. I tell you, it helped. It was all grist to the mill. I grew and grew in self-esteem. Best of all on a Thursday, when the queues were much shorter at the bakery, Wednesday being the day of general enlistment, as you never failed to tell me with that knowing look of yours. Man of bright-shining medals, every one bought at the shop. You are – how would I sum you, puzzle? – a long French bean strung up on a wire, exposed to rain, wind, what have you. No wonder you have always disgusted me. A certain anchoring. Down below. That is the wish, the yearn, at gangplank's end, face facing down towards the mighty roar of the ocean. When the lights cannot offer favours any longer, when they are all quite helpless, prisoners of war in peacetime, when I reach out for your finger end and find a poke of dry straw jerking ceiling-ward. It is at such moments of this that I pity you. Not at all? you say. Gestures of disbelief. You are like a child in a nursery. How I do pity you.

The days are perfectly competent when they declare themselves, nothing more than that. Screwed into a block of wood, which is itself attached, somewhat precariously, to the window frame. No more than this need be allowed for. It is all perfectly adequate, as is speech when we open the month – aaaah! – just sufficient before passing on by, as quickly as the skipping toes permit. The wallpaper does not cover the walls – in the same way as your clothes do not cover the body. Buttocks exposed. Chipolata of a penis swinging from side to side like the slow tick tock tick of the clock. Fingers flailing around in the eager air. I could give you a box in which to conceal yourself – or perhaps, better still, a tidy lesson in humanity.

My boy, let me tell you this, as an aside perhaps. You forsook me by slipping out of your skin. The first question was pending, and you did a bunk. After that, you lived a life of the utmost jollity, liar. All this was left behind, all this strew, all this stench. It became the long, long aftermath, with the ballroom waltzes slowing to a dirge of tearfulness, asking where, where does it all fit in? Who made the promises in the first place? And who broke them with impunity? Questions of speed are neither here nor there. There is no bodily speeding any longer because there are no longer bodies to speed with. We have packed them away, quite neatly, in their long, dark, damp boxes. Now the running is with words, keeping pace with it all, beating on doors, upturning cars, besmirching the ugliest of faces, all so effortless and unconquerable. Were you to rise up after me? Had we quite determined the order? Not in the instant of an eye. In the asking there is much. More than much. In the asking there is always the final satisfaction, no more than that. To comb through the waves effortlessly. To cry out loud. To bite with the teeth provided. Splendid. Bright-shining.

It was all made possible by life's nonsense, its steady flow-through, its heady, all-too-soon-and-ready skip-along. Otherwise, the feet would have dragged on interminably, and we would not have fashioned a keen path for ourselves through the meadows, across the keen, cold bite of the glaciers, along the underworld tunnels of Castleton where the stalagmites threaten unremittingly. Little more than that if you are listening with at least half an ear cocked to me.

I suppose not then. You never asked, granted that. You never pleaded with me to enter. In fact, the door was blocked and there was never room enough even to approach. That was always made clear to us by the back-room boys, all that shifty-eyed nonsense, to which you were a party so willingly, and for so long. Did you scream just then? I heard a rent in the air, and it was not thunder. Something much lighter and easier on the ear, it has to be said, and so I said it. Who would not? I'm here after all, pacing it all out, first the breadth and then the length, wondering whether we can ever even happily live here together with two or three books and a stove to consider. Where were you when I took the final vow anyway? I never asked for you, and you refused to concede – which is, of course, entirely within your character.

Why always make it seem so difficult? Each of us has an entirely separate body, mine here, yours there. Isn't that enough to be said? Do you really need more? I could offer you a cheese scone from this side of the bed, but it is old, and barely registers a flicker when moved aside by the finger. Otherwise, there is always the tide to keep in order. Will you help me with that? You once said that you would. I don't know. It is only voices for the pleading, a few random, pluckable voices, relatively unknown I would say, relatively inconsequential. The world almost entirely consists of used car lots these days, and I am all for a little forbearance if we propose to go no further in this weather. It is your call, I would suggest. I am too ham-fisted, and the crampons have shattered. Did you not utter words in drifts, generally speaking? Or is it only snow that does that? I jest, of course. I have been too long at the easel, working up my plucky sprit, which has proven elusive again. Would you ask in my stead? I would give you something. Are you down to nine digits? Well then, that would be the answer to the state's improvidence, about which I care, I hasten to add, not one jot, babe of the moon sculls, as you have always been known to me in my inner recesses. It has been too long and too slow in coming. It always feels like filling in the gaps, as if there is always more to be said and you will be the one to say it, of course. Your pace was always swifter, jock. No. No matter. The curfew lingers again, and I must be going back to my pocket. It is simple in there, and small, and a little stinking. What usefulness then? Could you define a home by its walls, even in defiance of a firing squad? I would hesitate to call that an extreme circumstance because you have fired them up all over the backyard, and there is little left to shout down by our lights. I might beg to differ, but that is down to the two of us as usual, arm in arm once again with so little to lose, and very quickly too, my friend, my chastening helpmate.

Was it not the whale which carried you off in the end? And was it not subsequently found dead without you? And there was not even a note or the smallest smearing of blood. That is the way of you, always so clean-heeled and flighty. Always once too often for the rest of us, nifty. Are we then toothless? Could that be why the kingdom collapsed with a sigh? We gained nothing, I reckon. We gave it all away. Even the words dissolved into nothingness, would you not say? I hear a tearing of the carpet, which is too much and too many for me at this dawn hour, when the mist settles comfortably into the gully of the roof of the barn, and I swim over as usual to take my morning's fond ablutions. I am so strong when it is called for. I gain weight at a steady pace. And all France seems to welcome me, I would say, though not without exaggeration.

Were you giggling in the wings? Did you tear down the curtain? Is this as much as has been granted today, no more than this? Have you then turned into a makeweight or a shillyshallyer? I would gather all the scattered crumbs into a single pocket and hope for the best. Good fortune to stout breast bones! There is no other way. It will soon be yesterday. And what hope for us then, we who have scarcely begun? Not a prima donna. Too small for that, and too flimsy by half. There is a homestead needs filling with bunches of petunias at the door, reaching up and out with their necks. Such gawky presences. Fortunately, I made up for it all by just being there, in all the fullness of my worldly confidence, carrying a leather briefcase of course, which I swung gently from side to side as if I were a public convenience, equipped to be admired by all.

And then you just said no, no, no, as if you were the state's supreme law giver, and all else was so much blahty, blahty, blah. Who can countenance such stuff? Who would not readily put a match to it and walk briskly away as if going on holiday? Yours is just too much for me again (me and mine, that is), too many limbs spilling forth in all directions, too many bitter certitudes, which hold up and lock together like a series of long, metal bars that might sustain a new-build in, say, China, in fact any new-gleaming city of the kind we might never wish to enter, oh no. Do you get my drift? Are you flowing here with me, tidal-flowing I mean, not something far less serious? Has your hair let you down yet or did you shave it all off in too much of a hurry and say god damn and blast to all of them? I would not put it past you. Too many leaves gather between the furniture. They do catch at the throat. They plead their cause with such tedium, interminable murmurations of leaves, leaves, leaves, all lost and gone, all wrenched from the tree, tree, trees... Frankly, I would rather be a frog tidily adjacent to a stick or a browsing goat with an old grey beard and a book. Any of that would suit me better than this, all this tepid water to be wallowing in, and never any possibility of heating it up until doomsday or beyond. Perhaps, incidentally, that may be the test of doomsday in the end, that the water is finally heated up in that giant tub, and we all jump in, we great and unruly crowd of unknowings. Yippee!

Godliness is first cousin to unsightliness, you told me that as you stepped forth in your long johns, out at the knees and so pitifully craving attention. Undeserved to a man! And who is a man anyway?

I have looked in all directions. I have not seen one since the late war took the last survivor away, with happy cheering all round. And then this mood of settled desolation, I do feel. They did add something, though I am not quite sure what. A certain turpitude, godlessness, all those unmemorable hours of inconsequence as the last one drowned in his own blood? We would have carried him over our heads, down that final hill, had we been close by, but it would have meant travelling just before lunch, and all the trains were messed up, and even your cat, who is not usually a whiner, was bawling for food in the tray again.

I don't know what to make of it all. There is this wall again, and pins will not do, nor far-fetched notices. You hate us anyway, so what difference will a wall make to the general situation? We can toss buns over, the strong ones, the limber of arm, with little notes of consolation stuffed inside. Yes, let's do that before the Poetry Classes resume or we will be incapable of writing anything. Poets are like great storms brewing, you seldom get over them. See the extensive notes I wrote about all of this back along when the cooling streams were still happily gurgling.

The answer, of course, is to deal in long-term horse-trading, that is the answer by my lights, which are sputtering towards extinction in this mood of extreme melancholia which now grips me. All days are one now, it seems, and the bricks in the wall no longer add up, no matter how often we line up to count them. What is to be done? Ask Lenin. Ask that picture postcard of the mausoleum, fading now, and curling back on itself so shyly, which is tucked into the corner of your window facing the shingles. Let the teddy bear in his jaunty sailor hat croon him to sleep. Scarcely necessary. He is long dead already – like the rest of us.

I have none. I have looked and I have looked. I have looked everywhere, with a name to be known by. That thorough. It is no use badgering me. I refuse to become a victim of tinnitus. This rebel spark is sure to ignite again by and by, when we are all ready and upright and dressed, inclined to believe that new day is dawning. Cause and effect, that is all there is to it. We both know that. It is scarcely worth saying. You shoot out a foot, a single damp foot, and then you withdraw it again.

Is there any more to be said? How many repetitions would you like to pay for? They are relatively expensive at the weekends, less so on a Thursday, which is always my favourite because it begins to promise so much without being exactly specific. And who needs to have one's mouth crammed with specificity as if it were so much thick furnishing fabric? I have had enough of it. I go for clean living these days, and a small element of fastidiousness between the cracks, which I always attend to at first light if my finger ends are not numb again at waking. Does that mean I am suffering, that I have always been suffering? Of course not! Distract yourself. Become a tawdry man like the rest. There are only so many pairs of boots to go around.

Is your measure my monstrance or did I take it all amiss again as if I were in the grip of some familiar drunken stupor, and all the feral cats were rising as one to the kill? I would not believe it of you. Never. Lay down your coin beside mine on this table top by way of mutual reassurance. You are not that kind of a day. You have a cooling freshness about you, and that is all that there is to be said of you, I am sorry to say, because in the end you do bore me, and I must walk away with the golden calf stuffed in my pocket, a small simulacrum of the one we always loved, before the god of the Israelites roundly condemned us once again for being ourselves, alas. It is all so needful though. And so repeatable. Everybody knows so much these days, and especially those who are gifted with such profound ignorance. Why conceal the truth again? That is why there has been so much turmoil in recent years, with every door slammed shut. Mutual consternation. No one ever quite believed that it could turn out like this. Nor me. And I was the truest of true believers when in short trousers. No, no one could jump higher, no boy walk the floor, back and forth, in such a mood of civic well being. Wasn't that it? Or were they always baying for more? I wouldn't put it past them, the charlatans. Now what though? Is not that what you were asking? And if not that, well what? There are only so many questions, and I do become a little exhausted by evening. My pen does falter. I leak from every pore or crevice. There is never enough it seems. They are always crying out for more. Or there is always too much. What is it about us? Why not, mouths clothed, contentedly creep about this floor, this monastic space of ours, with the morn light leaking through our favourite round-headed window, in blissful silence? Would that not serve us all a little better in the circumstances, which are entirely of our own making? Ball it all up. Toss it away. Feed it to the dog.

I have always told you, have I not, that I am more than contented to be myself. It seems to me that there is no other option – or no other potion. There would be too much waste, too much leakage, too much disappointment, were I to boldly stride forth in an entirely different guise. All continuities would be lost. I would not know what to say. I would be obliged to begin again, on a different soap box altogether, and at an hour other than this one. Would not all times be scrambled? Would I have that to face too? Almost certainly. And in all likelihood you would not be there to egg me on, would you? It is as it is then. Wash our hands of it. Take it for null, nothing. There are many makeshift opportunities, and we are all hurriedly leaving at once, I guess, pulling on our heavy winter topcoats, so moth-eaten these days, because that is the end of it.

God help us all in the end! I for one could just stand here and weep. Were I a man of less mettle. Just look at me for god's sake. Look at all these rags and tatters. Quite shameful, I'm sure you'd agree. Who dragged us up like this, so shameless. My mother could barely look at me, she once said, at a moment of chilling honesty in my childhood. I told her I completely understood before grinding the thing out with my heel. Hang on though! Don't take liberties, madam! Well, why not? Who else to plead to? I am out here on my own, and you are over there – I know it, I can see you all, no point in pretending again – feigning a mild interest in all these odd antics of mine, which just seem to keep going on and on because, well, there is nothing else for it at our time of age, is there? I didn't ask to do it like this. We signed the papers, and that was it. And then one day, when I was taking my usual afternoon snoozy woozy with Stravinsky tootling on the horn somewhere, there was a rap on the door, and there you were – or one of your awful proxies more like – saying: where were you? We have only so much rehearsal time before the big night, you know. Another big night! I stuttered. Not another one, surely. Isn't the whole damnable thing over by now? And you said, finger-jabbing (I remember it to this day): who told you it was ever going to end until it really and truly ends? I just nodded. I felt like an animal trapped in a cage, with a searchlight playing across my terrorised pupils. And so here we are again, wobbling along, street-wise as they say, *street-*

wise (street-foolish more like) and trying one's level best not to fall off this time. We are alive, aren't we? Flesh and bone? Well then, all done and dusted. Mattocks to the fore! Sword clash in the night! Noises of tumult off! God in his heaven. Let the fol de rols continue, my sometime friend!

I couldn't lift them. I told the man. I pointed to the tiles, all those heaps of them. Teetering like that, stacked up and teetering in their heaps. I pointed up to the roof. He shrugged his shoulders. He turned away. What more is there to be said or done? It was a long time ago now. Except that it isn't. It's now. I am carrying them one by one, to the base of the wall of the barn, and then looking up. My hands are still trembling in anger. The truth is he left them there. We both left them there. We walked away. I heard the engine of his Peugeot van firing up in the lane. And then he quietly crept away, as if ashamed.

I had always wanted – and expected – the ending to be peaceful and *conclusive* because that is how endings are supposed to be. It was quite the opposite of peaceful. In fact, it was so lacking in peacefulness that no one – least of all myself – could determine whether it had really finished or not. It was all too ragged, too undetermined, too all over the place. There was too much going on, too much mayhem – people zizzing about like disgusting fat bluebottles around a joint of meat – in all directions. Actors were forever arriving and pointing at their watches. Understudies were wondering aloud when they were going to be needed. The beefy sort in t-shirts who always heave the sets about were seizing hold of this, that and the other – much to my amazement because I had thought until that moment that we already *knew* the order of things, and that there are only certain props you can use before the final scene, minimal usually, as if to demonstrate that all this has at last fallen away, all life's jiggery pokery, all life's endless games – jousting with sticks and words and gestures, all that nonsense. And so here I was in the midst of it all again, more a beginning or a middle than an end, and people were coming up to me and asking *me* for guidance, as if I were expected to know what was going to happen next. Quite ridiculous. I'm just one of the players, I kept on saying it, shouting it almost. In what bar has the director chosen to hole himself up? Drag him out then. Let him show himself in front of us, the weasel. What are we paying him for anyway?

There is no such thing as the countryside any more. Have I said that yet? Do I regret its going? Not at all. The rural was always so unreal anyway. I never felt at home there. I never had any wish to be a sheep or a dog or to suffer in the way that animals do, to die in an abattoir, or to be shot on the wing for the sake of a second's passing amusement. That was never my idea of a perfect death. Above all, I have always loved the clean lines of those mighty A roads, the ones that cut through so with such ruthless directness and at such speed. I used to tell you all this, I remember, and you would cower away from me into the corner of your seat, almost trying to pretend that I had not said such a thing. You couldn't believe the speed at which I used to drive, the silly noises I would make when in the driving seat, the needlessly violent swings of the wheel. That is why you left me, because I was such a dangerous and irresponsible child. I had never stopped sucking my thumb, you said, drool streaming down my wrist like a baby. And so one day I did away with the countryside altogether. I set a match to France. That was not difficult. I merely had to extend a single arm across the Channel, light, and then blow, hard. It did the trick. The English were quite awe-struck – not all of them were friends of mine, needless to say. They had had it in mind to do something similar since about the thirteenth century, they told me. Why had they been so dilatory then? I asked, before raising a glass in a bar in south London. I choose to drink on my own, always. It is so much easier to let one's thoughts come together when one drinks on one's own, such a joy to contemplate the slow settling of the sediment. It did mean that I had lost it all, of course, all my France too, the part that I had owned and cultivated in my very small way beyond the window – the fig tree, the lavender bushes, my blazing green catalpa, those ever ripening and ever more succulent yellow cherries of early summer. Perhaps it did not matter. I still had my words for it all. Would it matter if I set those on fire too, if I expunged, at a stroke, all my known words and worlds, in order to leave myself in a condition of untrammelled emptiness? Would such purity appeal to me? They absented themselves one by one, the roof tiles. I watched them fall away, almost suicidally. Had they grown tired of being examined too carefully by my tender, scrutinising eye? Was that the problem? Could terracotta roof tiles be said to possess such feelings? In fact, they did not fall away at all. They lifted off, one by one, into the sky, laboursomely, like birds far too heavy for their own good, and they even flew a little way, toiling on their phantom wings, as far as... just beyond the garden's boundary wall, at which point they stopped, hovered for half a bated breath (mine, of course), and then plunged into the poppy field, and shattered. I watched the pieces rise up in a pother of dust, so slowly, as if so carefully orchestrated. I watched them go, one by one, quite unhurriedly, over a matter of days and weeks. I felt for their gestures. I knew what it would mean, those slow gestures of abandonment: the old barn itself would not be long in going. The unceasing rain has its wiles. It also bides its time.

As do I. And as do you too. We have been here for breaths far too many, walking these streets, sitting outside this café of ours – or theirs – in patient anticipation of the Saturday market, which will, we know all too well, come and go, and for the weather to come and go too, forever changing in its moods. The weather is all too humanly fickle. I have opened and closed this book, have I not, times innumerable. I know it through and through. I have inhaled, deeply, the smell of its pages. I have dreamt over and over of the man who owned it before me, and of how he lived. Not wholly dissimilar to a life such as mine. I may even have read it. It is my boon companion, the very same. I have closed it from time to time and walked away a pace or two, down to the pharmacy, which has just now closed for lunch, and so I may choose to go a little further, along that narrow street just to the left, no effort at all, so close to where the river waits in all its quiet wiles, beckoning us to go and look. The river, that which turns and turns in its bed, never quite sleeping, never quite waking. I go there, down to the very brink of the water, in order to admire the poplars on the opposite bank, and then I return to the café for my first glass of Pelforth of the day. It comforts me so. It settles me into myself. It enables me to forget that you have left me, oh only a little while ago, I tell myself, when you were of such and such an age, and entirely sweet and wholly admirable. You are walking back to me now from a great distance, and I am raising my glass to you, as I would always do in the garden, when you approached me with the tray and the second bottle. Here you come now. You have let your glance fall away, and now you have settled at another table. No, it is not you, I see that now. Someone has borrowed, for an instance, the look of you, your deportment. No matter. The day will not easily be deflected from its course. And I shall walk along in step, gradually, never hurrying, never hazarding too much because there is always too much to be hazarded, and that way lies ruin or condemnation. (Which though?) And we know all about that, my constant of days. Should we pool our resources, such as they are? Is that an option? Or would that be too much to ask of you? How much, in fact, would you want me to ask of you? You are a thin film. When I squeeze you between thumb and finger, there is nothing to you. By comparison, you would call me stout as a barrel.

I never made a final claim. You have mistaken me for someone else. I slept, oh, a good twenty-four hours before dragging myself out of bed, by which time all the men had gone, and the sky looked as threatening as ever, even before your final instruction to be gone because I had *outlasted your pleasure*, as you so deftly put it. Where do you find such phrases? They do not flatter you. I have never liked the cut of your jib. That is why we have always been antagonists. It could not have gone any other way. The park benches were cemented in by the council and there was no budging them. Don't tell me I didn't try, don't lob that insult at me because it will not wash. I have always been *clean living*. Would you like me to say it again? I have always settled my dues by life.

What did you say just then? Your sort would need a megaphone to reach me because I am beyond all that sort of thing. I move by a settled rhythm, a rhythm which seems to define me to my own satisfaction. Who needs more than that? Have you heard of the chrysalis, and of that which emerges if one chooses to show patience, patience? Well then, don't try to wrong-foot me with irrelevancies.

There was no wallpaper. By then, the rooms were at such and such an angle to the true. What is more, the faces are an irrelevance. You are lying to me. I made the furniture myself, long after I had begun to cultivate the forest because they were all mature trees, and the entire enterprise came about single-handed – just look at the state of these clothes! – because I am a brute of a man with a long, wild call. You were the dust between one board and another, easily swept away. I wouldn't call that an insult. I would describe it as hard fact. That is why, in my opinion, there is no space for your words in this tight-knit argument. My fluid words embrace the two of us, and the judge, set up there on his gleaming pedestal, will surely agree. Smoking on the back step will take us nowhere, you surely know that. You have tried it all before, with your hoodwinking, your brazen hoodwinking. Why do I need to ask anyone? I do not value a second opinion, that is what it all amounts to in the end. It is a question of integrity, and how I have shaped its meaning. You remember how a boat, when driven at speed across the lake, prow bucking as it goes, cuts through so magnificently? That is my paradigm. You stick to it too. It will serve us all well in the interim, before the main feature kicks in, and we set to again chomping down on the popcorn, just as if we were chums of yore. Well, we were that once, weren't we? Don't try to contradict that statement too!

This table could be divided cleanly in half if you insisted. I am dandling the saw in my hand. Just look at me now. Twist your head in this direction. Bother for a change! Would that be your last wish? Or will there be many others by and by, arriving by the sackful to torment me? I wouldn't put it past you. Send them by mountain goat, so fleet of foot, from rock to rock leaping, if you so wish. A goat can harry what little hair remains up top, can't it? Don't try to disguise the devilish intricacy of your twisted thinking. I have seen pictures from a village, supposedly described as primitive, showing such scenes. Recent? The negatives were far too wet to reach a judgement. What are we then in the end? And what in heaven's name are *you*? A spatchcock lily? No, I hate myself more than I hate you. Having to give account of oneself when there is so little to be said that is truly admirable, such is my curse. Count it on two fingers. No more than that. A chance greeting. The accidental gift of a word of praise or two. Who would begrudge that? I would. So little to be eked out, and over so many years of sad, hard toil. Who would countenance such a life had one been given the right to choose before descending the slippery chute? Into the dangerous world indeed, without hope, comfort or rest. Those were the poet's words of general condemnation, to be taken lightly, with a pinch of salt, or not at all. Beavers build dams, bless 'em.

In the kingdom there will be turrets, many. Should I go on a little further when the corn flakes are thirsting in the bowl? I pity them all, there is nothing to be excepted. The word is this: a rout. In the end I would say no, resoundingly, for what it is worth. And you would tag along behind, for all your protestations to the contrary. You would make up the numbers. It is what you do. You are a make-weight – when you are not swatting flies in the kitchen against the imminent threat of disease. Is your memory large enough to be contained within mine? Don't try to presume. That may be a request too many. So let me turn the tables on you by saying this: you take *me*. You pack me away, and then see what you make of all the glaring inconsistencies. You wouldn't keep me there for a single day. You would burn me. You would rend me. And that would be the least of my problems.

There was never time enough for just the two of us. How could there be? Were you just standing there, whistling idly? Shame on you, you paper brigand! Those between-times do come and go. Entr'actes, that's what they call them. Washing around here and there, as if nothing really mattered but the roaring now, now nowness of things. All so whizz-bangy. And all so fiddly technical too before the lights go up, finally, and someone steps up – the *leading man* is the derisory turn of phrase, I do believe – makes that single decisive gesture. Did you see it by any chance? Yesterday? Or did you dip into a doorway out of the downpour? My god, how glad I was to miss it all. I would have given anything but a five-barred gate, as the bushy-bearded farmers tend to say. Not that I know any. Not my patch. I'm a hard pavement man myself. Someone responds then – supposedly. It's a matter of a split second – here, then gone. On a knife edge from moment to moment, with the words unlisted up to that point. You won't find them. A show of arrogance will get you nowhere – as you are already aware. There is such high jinks about these days, such lack of reason to the way they hammer in the nails. Never top to bottom. Gloves too are a thing of the past. Why bother then? you might ask. All that's out the window, and sometimes even out there already – uninvited, uninvited, I say it once and then again for emphasis, I'm sure you'll understand – nonchalantly leaning on the parapet as if he or she – they alternate – owned the place. Any village street will do. With all the charm and all the nonchalance of high summer. Your low notes were always the ones that pleased me, as if you had merely drifted in without a second's thought, and I had embraced you like a hefty log tossed up from a river. The usual routine needless to say (why change it?), with music dribbling in from all four corners – should you have that many. I seldom keep much change about me. There is quite enough hereabouts for it to really matter, it seems to me. What give is there, ever, anyway? The portions are small and somewhat grudging, we always felt. There is nothing for it but to sit here though. There were scarcely other opportunities to be off and gone like the mudlark. I wouldn't have it any other way. That is what popular tunes do to you, they drill into you until you are nothing but an inter-connected series of yawning cavities. All fried and charred – which is, from a visual point of view, something of a disappointment. I'm disappointed anyway. I rather expected more of myself. I stand here now in my stockinged feet and I see myself asking: why? How? When? Whither? Well, who's to blame? These are opportunity days, that's what the band says when it pipes up. I just go along for the company. I don't really want to know anyone, not any more. How many miles did you say you had travelled just to get here? Don't exaggerate, you nincompoop. I have known too many, and each and every one of them has been a minor disappointment. Too few words. Too many. Nose over-elongated. Breathing too stuttery. Smile fatuous and inerasable. Solutions to immediate problems unrealisable. Money, lacking. Jaw, weak. Why didn't you just stay in bed? I asked the last one. She was in her bed when I said it, which proved to be a tad confusing. What is more, I didn't even know her just then. That came later – according to some. I wish I owned a juicer. Juicers do things with words that dictionaries have scarcely begin to dream about. That is their appeal.

Or two, if you wish. I do have the space in the old back scullery. Did you hear a song coming on just then? Me too. After all, it will be Christmas again soon.

A lift is the thing, from someone quiet and muscular, someone who is not getting you down from the moment you wake up. There are such people, I believe, I have heard them spoken of at second hand, though they do tend to be expensive and, generally speaking, spoken for, the good ones that is. The range is enormous, like the span of an eagle's wings. Would you be partial to a flight or two up there in the aether? Mark it down as a hypothetical question – or of little me winging it in the guise of a comic, ha diddly ha ha – if the very idea terrifies you. Next up may be the town hall ghost because we are looking for something catchy to get us all going again, having been miserable now for weeks. Did you come along for a bit of glad-handing too that evening? Do I recognise your face? Of course I do. I have had enough of it though, by which I mean all this standing around, all this revving of the engine without actually releasing the brake. It sits on your head like a lead hat on an Edwardian beau. Were there such things? Was it too late by then? I have been one, though only by pretending. The trick is to say nothing, to let it happen without a mouse's squeak of protestation. Don't show off your weaknesses in that way. They will be far too ready to call you out. It's a bit like having over-baggy trousers, perfectly useless when the time comes to re-invent yourself as a minnow or a long-playing record of Shakespeare, locked up with some man-woman in a steamy closet. Such a lot of goodness seeps away without the least consequence. I have trained myself, doggedly, to bide my time or to go over-easy – which is what an egg does these days, though not in mine.

Down valley – as far as one call tell – the horses have gathered again. In fear or excitement? A little of the two? I wouldn't go near them. I would stick to the television if I were you. There is less risk of a broken limb. Make of it what you will. Dry ice melts too. There is just no stopping this spate of derelictions. It is filthy – and fearful. I booked a ticket the other day. It seemed to be the only way out of here. To risk it all. To throw it all a little way ahead and then to run after it, hell for leather. That will take some doing. I will have to ratchet up all those promises to myself!

About the author

Michael Glover is a Sheffield-born, Cambridge-educated, London-based poet and art critic, and poetry editor of *The Tablet*. He has written regularly for *Hyperallergic Weekend*, the *Independent*, *The Times*, the *Financial Times*, the *New Statesman* and *The Economist*. He has also been a London correspondent for *ARTNews*, New York. His latest books are: *Late Days* (2018), *Hypothetical May Morning* (2018), *Neo Rauch* (2019), *The Book of Extremities* (2019), *What You Do With Days* (2019), *John Ruskin: a dictionary*, and *Thrust: a spasmodic history of the cod-piece in art* (2019)

What other poets and critics have said about Michael Glover's poetry:

'Much energy and brio' – Seamus Heaney, Nobel Prize in Literature, 1995

'Michael Glover's lines unspool gravely and efficiently with few commas – like waves that know they are on their way to someplace, but without making much fuss about it. They can be piercingly sad and hilariously wry, sometimes at the same time. Michael Glover is a major find.'   – John Ashbery

'Michael Glover gives us, often dazzlingly, the poet as performer, conjuror, clown, operating with a playfulness which, whether putting forward arguments about language, reality or poetry itself, is artful and frequently highly enjoyable.' – Laurence Sail, *Stand*

9 781999 644093